The
Mutinous
Wind

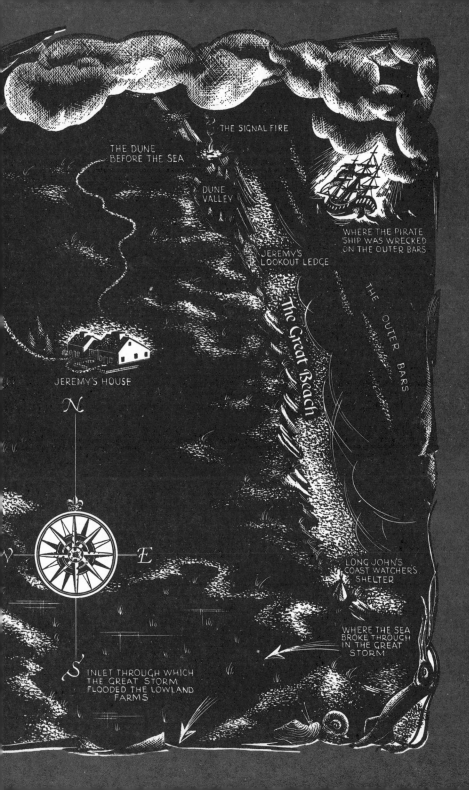

THE SIGNAL FIRE

THE DUNE
BEFORE THE SEA

DUNE
VALLEY

WHERE THE PIRATE
SHIP WAS WRECKED
ON THE OUTER BARS

JEREMY'S
LOOKOUT LEDGE

THE   OUTER   BARS

The Great Beach

JEREMY'S HOUSE

N

W   E

S

LONG JOHN'S
COAST WATCHER'S
SHELTER

WHERE THE SEA
BROKE THROUGH
IN THE GREAT
STORM

INLET THROUGH WHICH
THE GREAT STORM
FLOODED THE LOWLAND
FARMS

Books by Elizabeth Reynard

THE NARROW LAND

THE MUTINOUS WIND

The Mutinous Wind

by
Elizabeth Reynard

Illustrated by William Barss

PARNASSUS IMPRINTS
Orleans, Massachusetts

To
V. C. G.

who went with me
through the marsh

"And ye that on the sands with printless foot
Do chase the ebbing Neptune . . .
                    . . . by whose aid —
Weak masters though ye be — I have bedimm'd
The noontide sun, call'd forth the mutinous winds
And twixt the green sea and the azured vault
Set roaring war . . . "

THE TEMPEST, V. I. 34

Prefatory Note

VARIANTS of this story have been narrated at Cape hearthsides for two hundred years. The folklore upon which the tale draws is traditional to the towns of Eastham and Orleans (Eastham South Parish). The central figures, a pirate, a witch and the Sand Dobbies, may be found recorded in *The Narrow Land, Folk Chronicles of Old Cape Cod*, which I wrote some years ago.

Unlike that book, in which the destinies of the Sand Dobbies are not interwoven with the lives of Black Bellamy and the Sea Witch, and in which each tale is centered on one significant character and is recounted in a manner akin to the way in which it was told in its heyday, here I have undertaken to fuse a number of oral and written traditions into a single narrative. This story, therefore, is fiction, containing elements of both the earlier and later forms of Cape balladry and folklore.

As told by the elder generations, Cape yarns frequently moved at a lively rhythmic pace. They were a sort of prose balladry, a clipped and lilting prose, and made use of brief, recurrent phrases in the manner of the old ballads. Something of this sort I have attempted at moments in the story, relying in part on my memory of yarns told by my sea-captain grandfather and his seafaring friends.

Many seeming inconsistencies are of deliberate intent, such as the variable use of *ye* and *you,* presented with the conviction that such variations are natural to the story. The use of *ye,* for instance, was until the twentieth century a habit of the seagoing populace who thought of it less as an "old-fashioned" word than as a sign that one spoke a real sea lingo. My grandfather used *ye* now and again in talking to his sailors, but never when he desired to emphasize the pronoun, and never to my grandmother. She never used it at all.

A few words no longer current are used in the narrative. Most of these, such as *Coast Watcher,* explain themselves. The terms *Old Comer* and *blaze-away hole* may need definition. Old Comer was used to describe those of the New England pioneers who came in the first ships (1620–30). A blaze-away hole was a small opening in solid wooden window shutters through which a musket might be thrust to defend the house from attack.

Of the characters in the story, the pirate, Sam Bellamy, is the only historical figure. With him I have taken some of the liberties of authorship. The witch, Maria Hallett, I have not been able to authenticate as having been accused of witchcraft in any official document, but she is a well-known figure of legend on the Cape and there are several women of that name in the local town records.

The Sand Dobbies of Eastham are traceable in their family tree to the stable elves of Yorkshire, but Cape traditions have so far adapted them into the American scene that they have lost many of their Old World characteristics and they are one of the few if not the only fairy folk that we may rightly call our own.

The story has not been sifted of its haunting, antique mystery. To the modern reader its events may seem to move in the realm of extreme fantasy, but if he will pause and think of occurrences recent in our history, he will realize that the world of today is equally weird and mysterious.

Contents

Prologue
on
the Sea

Prologue on the Sea

In DAYS when ships unfurled their wings and skimmed over the bluewater and sheered along the sea lanes, a dark pine tree island stood in the center of a treacherous swamp. The swamp was a saltmarsh inlet on the Great Sea Hook, Cape Cod. And over the green-gold reeds of it a pale and airy mist hovered, a luminous sun-shot fog.

Men took this mist for a mooncast that lingered over the treachery sands as a mercy-warning of death. But some of the ancient seadogs swore that the mist was a sign of buried treasure — for those were the days when the Indies pirates plundered our coast, sank our vessels, captured our young seamen, then sailed away to the Southern Islands to gamble their stolen gold.

Those were the days when the Cape fishing fleets sailed to the North in spring. And in lean years, along with the fleet, merchantmen lacking cargoes sailed, to fish their own catches, salt them, stow them, then trade them in the West Indies for spices and Jamaica rum.

So as night came over the Grand Banks, alive with stars and the moving of water, Captain Snow of the sloop *Abigail* put a double watch in her crow's-nest and drew his vessel closer to the other small craft from home. Sailors below were muttering stories of a new pirate hero. Rich as a king and as easily cruel, a moody, dark-browed tempest of a man, he could out-sail every shipmaster in Christendom, outwit the King's vessels sent to pursue him, outfight with rapier, pistol or cutlass any man reckless enough to challenge him in open fight. The Black Bellamy he was called and came of the great seafaring stock bred on the coasts of Devon.

Through the long, idle hours of darkness the little fishing fleet from Cape Cod made lantern-talk with the Breton sailormen new from the French coast:

"Blink, blink," went the lantern language. "Have you heard about Sam Bellamy? He has taken the ship *Whidah*. The crew are in irons, chained belowdecks. The old captain is dead."

"What ship is she?" asked a Gloucester fisherman. Gloucestermen never get about.

"The loveliest ship on the Seven Seas, the 'Paradise Bird,' with teakwood decks and a carven poop. She can outsail a Man-o'-War. And we have heard tell that Bellamy swears he will sail her up the Colony Coast to plunder all Cape Cod."

"Stuff and nonsense," blinked back the lanterns of the Cape's fleet. "What would *he* want of the Great Sea Hook? *We* have no Spanish treasure."

"Men in the Island taverns say he comes for love of a lady."

"Tarradiddle yarns!" laughed the Cape sailors. "You Frenchmen are crazy!"

"Crazy or not, take heed! be warned!" answered the Breton seamen. "We heard it straight from the Island taverns, up from the ports of Spain."

Captain Snow had a full catch in the hold of the ship *Abigail*. Also down in the hold was chained a small white dog. The Captain had traded his gold brooch with a Scotsman for this pup, to be a come-home-from-the-sea present for his only son, Jeremy.

With the spring catch ready to be salted, the Captain turned the *Abigail* south, toward the Cape's sea hook and a little house that stood alone in the Dune Country by a misty marsh in the center of which, like the dark heart of a golden flower, rose up the Secret Island.

Far to the southward another captain, his vessel

laden with ivory and indigo, elephants' teeth and gold dust, sugar and Jesuits' bark, hoisted the Jolly Roger, the black flag of piracy, and headed the carven, golden prow of the loveliest ship in all the world up the sea lanes toward Cape Cod.

Far away in the tropic seas brooded the mutinous wind.

The Book
of
Maria

1

The Jeweled Chest

Wʜᴇɴ the principal kingdoms of earth seek domin-
ion over each other, they turn to alchemical wizardries
as today they have turned again. At a time when the
portents and powers of these were less veiled and far
less ominous, a little, dark-cloaked man of Spain com-
pounded a potion, sealed in a vial, locked in the till
of a jeweled chest that he carried under the folds of his
cloak aboard a Spanish galleon. The galleon put out
to sea. Her vast sails billowed; her black guns gleamed;
and she set her course for the far, bright coast of the
wilderness, America. There she was laden with fabu-

lous treasure, deck upon deck piled high with loot, and by night she sailed through the Windward Passage winging her way toward Spain.

The galleon rode high in the water; yet her watch in the night mist failed to discern a little Cape vessel, the *Flower of the Horn,* Captain Hallett in command. Born to fog, the Cape Cod captain slid his ship — silent as a ghost — under the galleon's guns. Then with knives in their teeth and pistols in their hands, the Cape men boarded the Spanish vessel, cut her halyards loose, killed her watch at their stations, and fought her deck by deck.

She was a carven palace of a ship; guns at every port; deck fighters in armor; gentlemen in broidered coats feasting in her gilded cabin. Before these had drawn their long Tagus blades, close-quarter fighting on the deck was done and Captain Hallett of Eastham Parish had captured a Spanish galleon.

But his luck did not hold. A squall arose, a *trapado* the seamen called it. The heavy galleon, her slashed sails whipping, was caught broad abeam and overset.

Cape men and Spanish wallowed alike in the spume-white walls of water. The stand-by crew of the *Flower of the Horn* fished what they could from the roiling ocean. Captain Hallett was saved and half his boarding crew, the Spanish captain and twenty of his men. But the treasure bound for the Court of Spain sank into the sea with the galleon.

When dawn came over the Windward Passage, for leagues on the water wreckage floated: bodies of Spaniards and Peninsula men, broad sails cut loose and like white whales fluking, stoven bolts, silken stuffs, and now and again a wooden chest built tight and riding the waves.

One of these chests drifted alongside and attracted Captain Hallett's eye. A small wooden box encrusted with jewels, it sparkled in the after-light of storm. The hearts of Peninsula men rose up. They thought it was a chest of treasure.

A seaman dove into the green sea maw and fastened a rope around the chest. It was hoisted aboard and Cape men and Spaniards crowded around while Captain Hallett sprung its ancient, rusty lock. When the lid was lifted the waiting sailors gave a low cry of chagrin. Here were no bars of yellow gold, no pieces of eight, no sparkle of gems. Only a pile of yellow-leaved books lettered in a fine hand.

The captain of the galleon recognized the chest. It belonged, he said, to an old man who had signed papers as a chartmaker, one of the many now asleep in the green meadows of the ocean.

The Spanish captain turned away from the Cape shipmaster and his crew, lest this spawn of Albion, these renegade heretics, witness his deep despair. Old was the Empire, old the galleon whose gold encrusted banners sank at the peaks of her sea-worn masts —

yet his Spanish heart still quickened with pride and clung with a fierce remembering faith to the gallant and unwieldy craft once the great Armadas of the Sea.

*   *   *

When the *Flower of the Horn* anchored in Province-town Harbor, Captain Hallett hired a post horse and strapped to its back the jeweled chest lashed in a sail-cloth cover. From among his crew he chose Sam Bellamy, a black-eyed sailor of the Devonshire Coast.

"Look ye, Sam," said the Captain, "I ride by stage from here to Eastham, thence across the pine tree country to Hallett House in the South Parish some mile from the King's Highway. Can ye ride a horse?"

"Aye, aye," said Sam.

"Then board this nag and follow the coach. As we pass through Wellfleet Settlement, mind ye, there will be toll to pay. The token given as payment of toll is a silver Spanish coin. This you will hold in your pocket, Sam, and relinquish it to no man until we leave the place. Elsewhere answer no challenge. And if the eyes of Wellfleeters bulge at sight of the chest strapped to your saddle, draw cutlass forth; ride close to the coach. Wellfleeters be a pack o' sea robbers spoiling for a quarterdeck brawl."

The black-eyed sailor grinned. "I have heerd tell," said he slyly, "that Wellfleeters speak much the same of the men from Eastham Parish."

The two set forth on a May morning. Dew was

bright on the Dune Country. The sea was spangled like a peacock's tail, but the coach wheels sank in heavy sand and the pull up the Hill of Storms was long. At Truro Tavern the travelers alighted to wet their throats with Canary wine and to tell the news of the Seven Seas to the old, shorebound captains.

In late afternoon the coach reached Eastham. The Captain climbed down from his seat on the top, bearing a bonnet box in his hand. He unstrapped his sea chest from the rear of the coach and a small wooden box with three new shawls in it, one red, broidered with gold, for his young daughter Maria, one blue with white silken flowers for her cousin Abigail, one gray with a sprig pattern for his sister-in-law Samantha who cared for the two girls. The bonnet was a howdy one, with roses under the brim. He devoutly hoped that Eastham Parish would have no notion of its price.

Homecoming is hard for a man when his wife is gone and there's no one left with whom to share voyaging memories. All his love centered now in the fair-haired girl, Maria, who so closely resembled his wife that sometimes, in glow of firelight, or the moon's tranquil radiance, it seemed as if the dead were risen to anchor again in life's harbor.

The young sailor drew in his horse. "Where away, Captain?" he inquired cheerily looking no whit the wearier for his long plodding ride.

"To Hallett House," said Captain Hallett, "a square-rigger built by my grandfer. The front door was sent over from England from the old house in Devonshire. My grandfer never could stomach the fancy that this new land was home."

"Devonshire," mused Bellamy, " 'tis the land I hail from, sir. Ten generations of us at the least have been bred to bluewater craft."

At Higgins Tavern Captain Hallett procured a second horse. He strapped to its saddle his own sea chest and the bonnet and shawl boxes. Then the two men made their way across country to a square house with wide chimneys set staunchly at either end of its steeply sloping roof. A brick walk led down the front and candlelight gleamed in the unshuttered windows. A Devonshire hedgerow rimmed a posy bed and bordered the green turf.

" 'Tis a chatterfest!" exclaimed the Captain, observing the lights in the windows with sudden gloom in his eye. "Samantha Doane who keeps house for me is no expender of tallow."

As he spoke, the front door was flung wide open. "Father, father," called a soft, young voice, and a girl with shining corn-colored hair ran down the steps and along the path and flung herself into the Captain's arms.

"For what is the front parlor lit?" he demanded, with a mock ferocious frown.

" 'Tis lit for *you*," said Maria. " 'Tis lit for your return."

"How knew ye that?" asked Captain Hallett. "Two

days ago with the winds against me I knew it not myself."

"Long John brought news of your ship, father, as it sailed upcoast past the Dune Country. So I figured the winds, and the course of the tides, and decided the hour of your coming."

"Spoken like a sailor," said the Captain. "What think ye of my daughter, Sam?"

The young Devonshire seaman loomed large in the sun's afterlight. He smiled but he spoke no word.

"He's shy," said the Captain. "He's afreed of women. But Sam's a good sailor, the best they make. And he's brought ye a present aboard that gray nag."

The Captain followed Maria into the brightly lighted house. Sam tied the horses to a hitching post, unlashed the canvas from the jeweled chest, carried it into the greatroom and placed it beside the hearth. As the firelight flickered on its carven lid the red rubies gleamed and the turquoise shone a deep green blue like Maria's eyes as she knelt beside the chest. With her young face alight in the ember glow, she looked to Sam Bellamy, who gazed at her long, like a small and eager angel waiting for the trumpets to sound.

"When may I open the chest, father? Is there aught to discover inside?"

"Naught that the world cares for, Maria. I would it were piled with jewels, or silken stuffs for your decking. But 'tis even as the sea gave it up to me, borne out of a foreign land."

Maria lifted the lid of the chest and pulled out a vellum-leaved book.

"What does it say?" asked her father curiously as her shining head bent over the close-written blacklettered pages.

" 'Tis a book of sorcery writ in Latin."

She pulled out another volume.

"What does that say? Is it Lucifer's words? Shall I cast it into the flame?"

" 'Tis a book of spells writ in the same tongue, but 'tis all white magic, not black."

Maria had learned to read Latin under the Reverend Mr. Samuel Treat, Minister of the South Parish, one of the learned disputants from England trained in a Cambridge College.

"Put the books away!"

Sam Bellamy spoke — suddenly — in a harsh voice.

Maria turned and gazed up at the tall sailor whose eyes were snapping, whose tanned cheeks were flushed.

"What say you, sir?" she queried mischievously.

"I said," said Sam turbulently, "put the books of witchcraft by!"

He had scarcely spoken when a rustling of skirts sounded on the stairway as Samantha Doane came down.

"Good evening, Captain." She paused a moment and glanced toward the young sailor.

"This be Sam Bellamy, Samantha, bred to the sea, an

Old Country lad. He'll make a great captain in his day."

He turned to Sam. "We sail this ship with a crew of four," said he. "There's Maria here, and her young cousin Abigail, orphaned by the waves and a right sweet girl. Then there's Samantha and me. Which of the two of us commands is a matter of some dispute. We'll put ye aloft in my searoom, Sam, where there's charts and a hammock more smooth-swinging than any landman's bed."

"Thankee, sir," said the sailor courteously, "but I plan to return to Eastham Tavern. 'Tis a matter of a fortnight till we sail again and Eastham is more to my liking than the roistering Province Lands."

"As ye will," replied the Captain, "but before you leave you must savor a wing of Samantha's roast Cape turkey, and drink a glass of her wine."

"That I shall gladly do," said Sam, and after a dinner spread fit for a king he mounted the horse from Higgins Tavern and leading the post horse by its bridle he rode in the gray-green night of spring back toward Eastham Town. A pale moon shone high in the sky, up over the distant sea. He smiled at it and he spoke aloud. " 'Tis a good-looking moon ye be tonight. 'Tis well ye're up apiece. For I aim to go courting this week," said he, "and I'll be needing your aid."

*   *   *

The week went by. Another passed. Captain Hallett rejoined his ship. But Sam was ailing from a chincough and an up-again-down-again fever. He coughed hollowly. He shook a little. He proclaimed that he had the ague.

"Mayhap a mite of chindoodle is cockcrowing under his breastbone," said Aunt Samantha dourly, "but he's also got light in his eye."

Before he left for the Indies, Captain Hallett doused this light.

"Maria's too young yet, Sam," said he. "You must leave her be till she's past sixteen. Come if ye must when I'm ashore, but when I'm afloat 'tis no part of a man to hang about petticoat doorstones."

Upstairs in the wide poster bed shared by Abigail and Maria, Maria poured forth her hopes and woes to her cousin who was wiser and gentler by a matter of three long years. Already Abigail had plighted troth to young Caleb Snow, a village captain, with a ship of his own and a fortune in land, a match approved by Aunt Samantha and fostered by Captain Hallett.

"Abigail," said Maria, her eyes shining, her small hands clenched, "you must help me to deceive them. I *must* see Sam! For I love him truly and he, I know, loves me."

Abigail, young and earnest, was torn between a strong sense of honor and decorum, and a fierce loyalty for little Maria whom she loved with the protecting and abetting love that ofttimes develops between two such motherless lonely children. She was afraid for Maria. Yet she shared to the full her cousin's admiration for the upstanding sailor from the Old Country whose courteous manners and lively temper seemed to her to match surpassing well with the quicksilver girl he was courting.

The two cousins went to bed betimes to the gratification of Aunt Samantha. Then Abigail assisted Maria to climb down the trellis of vines by the window, a connivance granted in return for a promise that Maria would not go twenty steps past the turn of the Devonshire hedge.

Beyond the hedge Sam Bellamy waited and the two talked and dreamed of the future. Sam was only a seaman, though apprenticed to learn navigation and ship lading under a skillful captain. And in those days of lagging trade his chance for a ship was slim. "If only, if only," he said to Maria, "I had loan of a wallowing coaster. I know where there's treasure to salvage, my darling, treasure fit for a queen."

Over and over again he told her of the Spanish galleon that her father had taken, of how it sank in the Windward Passage at a point that young Sam charted carefully on a Navigator's sheet. He told her how on his first voyage he had learned to salvage sunken gold, sailing from Plymouth to an island off Tripoli where, with the aid of African divers, he had helped raise bullion from an English ship sunk by the Algerine pirates.

"Could you not combine fortunes," asked Maria, "with one who has a shallow-draft vessel, one who would share the spoils?"

"I share the gold with no man," answered Sam. "The treasure is meant for *you*."

"But Sam, we shall grow old and gray. We shall never be married, if you have no ship. In five years I shall reach a score and that is a very old maid."

"In the West Indies," said Bellamy, "there are cut-throats capturing trader ships under the Black Flag. I am tempted to go on the account and win me a ship by the power of my cutlass. For I am a fighter, Maria. All men fall before me."

At that, Maria cried aloud in fear, so he took her in his arms to comfort her.

And up in the bedroom of Hallett House, Abigail, white-faced, prayed on her knees for the cousin whom she adored. Minutes seemed hours while Maria was away. All the Pitfalls of Hell that old Mr. Treat described so well of a Sunday thronged through Abigail's mind. Then she heard the noise that was not the wind in the trellis vines by the window and up crawled Maria with bright pink cheeks and shining eyes and with about her no faintest look of having consorted with the Devil.

Captain Hallett returned from his voyage. When he heard that Sam Bellamy was still at the Tavern, he took a horsewhip from the stable and walked along the pine-tree path to the door of Higgins Tavern. In the

taproom taverners said that Sam was down in the
Apple Tree Hollow below the Burying Acre, where
he loved to walk of a night. Into the Hollow strode
Captain Hallett. There he found the dark-eyed sailor
seated on a wooden bench. The droop of the boy's
shoulders smote him, and he thought of his own pinch-
penny youth when he had wooed young Maria Doane
in that same Apple Tree Hollow. The boy did not
hear his approaching steps, and started violently when
the Captain laid a hand on the bent shoulders.

"Sam," said the Cape Captain gently, " 'tis time you
went to sea. There's a deal o' talk in the Parish. If 'tis
truth they tell, I'll lash ye for it. But you are young
and in matters of love have given no trouble before.
Samantha tells me you've kept fair distant. Abigail
and Maria, she says, have gone to bed prompt of a
night. So I disbelieve the village tales and bid ye rejoin your ship."

Sam stared at the Captain. "In your day, sir, there
was chance for a man. Now, without schooling or
money or a ship, how shall I make my fortune?"

"I have no son," said Captain Hallett. "In all the
world I have only this daughter. The mate of my ship
is an old man now, nigh done with seafaring. I will
give ye his berth when the time comes and when you
have savings and build up a house, then if she wills,
you shall wed Maria, as a freeman of Eastham Parish."

"I am English born," replied Samuel Bellamy, "and
little concerned with hot-tongued matters of bishops'

and parsons' dispute. I am English bred on England's ships. I am a Devonshire man."

Then Sam told the Captain how he chanced to be skilled at salvage, how he charted leads over the sunken galleon, how he knew that she lay in a calm water not too far beneath the sea's surface for a diver of courage and strength. He begged the Cape captain to join with him in the raising of gold from the ship.

Captain Hallett was trader born. He had no faith in the sea's return of what it takes away. "Run the vessel aground," he muttered. " 'Tis not worth the risk, young Sam. Earn your money by trade, I tell ye, in the way of the new Americas. 'Tis the destined life of the Colony."

Sam drew his dark brows together.

"Your wits are gone flapping like crows, sailor," continued the Captain severely, discerning signs of rebellion and the quick discredance of youth. "There's naught in your plan but a broke back, a stove ship, and goodmen to mock ye in every tavern on the coast."

*   *   *

That night Maria met her lover.

"What says he, Sam, about us?"

"He bids me go to sea, Maria — bids me work till I'm old and you be, too. Then he says when he's dead, in forty year, you and I might get married."

"What of the Spanish treasure?"

"He says 'tis wing-flapping folly of youth. He says that he'll have none of it."

"Are you going to sea? Shall you leave me, Sam?"

"Aye, Maria, I'll sign on now with the *Flower of the Horn* for her southerly voyage, but as soon as she reaches the Indies, I'll go on the account."

"Sea robbers be sinful men."

"Yea, the cutthroats of the Seven Seas have scant hope of a king's pardon, but at least they be men of courage. Among them I'll find one with far sight, one with a ship and a venturesome spirit, one who will help me to raise at least the bars of gold from the galleon."

"The *Flower of the Horn* sails in two days."

"Only two days, Maria?"

"And I dare not see you again, Sam. Father is smarter than Aunt Samantha. The vine outside the window looks over-worn for the season."

They said good-bye with a wistful passion, the youthful love that suddenly leaps to a very bright blaze and then goes blind to the gathering darkness round it.

That night when Maria returned from her tryst, she crept downstairs to the chest by the hearth. From the chest she took a book of spells and carried it up to her bedroom.

"What have you there?" asked Abigail.

"'Tis one of the books of sorcery. My heart aches. My spirit is broken. I cannot sleep this night."

"Your father tells me," said Abigail, "that he's offered Sam a berth on his ship and a chance to rise in the trade. What more could man ask than that? After a space when you, like me, are of suitable age for wedlock, then you and Sam will get married. I see nothing to burn tallow about, or lie awake in the night."

Abigail turned on her side so the candlelight would not shine in her eyes and soon she fell asleep. But Maria sat reading the ancient book till dawn came in at the window. As she read, her eyes grew large with wonder, her cheeks paled, her hands trembled; and she looked so wan in the morning light that Captain Hallett talked at great length about cargoes from the Indies and how he and Sam together might venture a stake in the Boston trade.

Maria listened abstractedly. She kept eyeing the path to the rear of the house, and when about noon she heard a soft footfall, she rushed to the summer kitchen and out the door to encounter Long John before he came into the house.

"Long John, I have need of your help."

Long John gazed at her gravely. He was a Coast Watcher, but he was also a Doane Indian, born and bred to service in the house of Mr. Justice Doane, who was Maria's grandfather. He felt a particular duty toward Samantha and her niece.

"I like not your look," said he.

"Will you help me, Long John? Will you go to the Tavern and give this note to the sailor, Bellamy?"

Long John peered at her closely. "Is this against your father's wish?"

"Aye," said Maria, "but I love Sam truly, and this note only tells him a way in which he may win him a ship."

"I will deliver your message," said the Indian, "to the Bloodbrother of the Devil, but he will bring you no joy, Maria. He will bring you no peace."

"I shall never have peace without him, Long John. 'Tis writ thus in the stars."

"If you were a squaw," said Long John the Indian, "you would be whipped with your father's whip. But as you are only a white man's daughter, you will have your way and suffer. I would that you were a squaw."

2

The Ship Lilith

AFTER the nooning meal was over Maria slipped quietly out the door and took the path to the stable. There she saddled her father's horse and mounting astride with her skirts disarranged and her ankles showing, she rode rapidly over the hill.

Abigail saw her go. Abigail's knees were sore from praying but she sank right down on the pantry floor and beseeched the Lord to be prompt.

Skirting the town of Eastham, Maria made her way through green pine woods toward the long blue line of the sea. After about an hour's ride she came to the edge of a reedy swamp. Here she dismounted and tethered her horse. Before her stretched a level expanse of yellow reeds and green-gold grasses and quiet, shimmering pools. In the center of these stood an island whose tall pines rose like a pinnacled fortress above a delicate amber mist that hung, though the day was elsewhere clear, over the silent marsh. Suffused with gold, this gossamer air had a woven look like the ribbons of cloud when the rays of the sun draw water.

Maria took off her buckled shoes. Her stockings she thrust in her pocket. Then feeling the warm smooth sand with her toes she ventured out on a narrow bar that curved toward the center of the marsh through dark mud-holes and quagmire. Soon the bogs on either side of the bar were replaced by walls of swaying reeds taller than Maria's head. As the path twisted its way through these, no one from shore who gazed at the swamp would believe that mortal passed through it.

For a full half-turn of the hourglass Maria followed the hidden path till she came to a wide and shallow pool, sea-green at its shadowy edges, blue-green at the center. It gleamed in the golden setting of the marsh like a giant fallen India opal with a fluctuant fire that moved in its depths tindered by the flaming sun.

Maria lifted her soft gray skirts and waded through the pool. Soon after, she came to a small sand beach that rimmed the dark pine-tree island. At the head of the beach a boulder stood like a sentinel keeping long

watch. On the top of this boulder a huge scored shell
heaved itself upward and a leathery head with lidded
eyes protruded over the stone.

"Good day to ye, Snake-eye," said Maria Hallett.
The old sea turtle hissed.

In the center of the island a stout stockade surrounded a tiny daubed house. Here, in the early days
of the Colony, when rumors came of Indian raids, the
Doane men hid their women and children, their gold,
their kettles and tools. Only one path, safe from the
quicksands, led through the marsh to this island and
only the Doanes and Long John the Indian knew this
hidden way.

Maria entered the old-time hut and barred its ancient door. The greatroom, for such was the name that
Cape folks gave to the room where they cooked, ate
and lived, was flanked by two small bedrooms, an upstep room where the eaves sloped low, where the floor
was raised to allow space beneath for a small circular
cellar, and a downstep room for master and mistress
which still contained a high poster bed palleted now
with straw. At one side of the greatroom an oak ladder led to a storage loft, and opposite the entrance
door a wide, old hearth with an inglenook still held
banked ash from fires.

Maria seated herself on the settle and pulled on her
stockings and shoes. Next she produced from capacious
pockets a score of pages torn from her Bible, a flint and

tinder, a looming needle, and a sharpened goose quill. Striking fire, she burned to an ash the pages of the Holy Book. Pricking her finger, she let fall from it drops of her blood on the heretic ash. Taking the sharpened quill in her hand she dipped it into this Heart's Blood Ink and slowly and with frequent redippings of the quill inscribed the words *Maria Hallett* on the first page of the book.

The clouds that were over the sea thickened. A dense fog crept toward the Secret Island. Over her head a whirring sounded as an owl on the rooftree startled from slumber flew past the old stockade.

A soft knock came at the door.

"Who waits?" quavered young Maria.

"'Tis only I." The gentle voice seemed hesitant and tremulous. Tiptoeing to the shuttered window, Maria peered through a blaze-away hole and beheld on the doorstep a little old man clad in a long dark cloak. So frail, so bent, so old he seemed, leaning there on his gnarled gray stick, that no one could be afeered of him, so Maria unbarred the door.

"How did you get to this island, Gaffer?" Her question was breathless with boding.

"I came by a path that I knew of yore." The old man smiled serenely. "I be one of the Colony Old Comers, lass. Will ye not let me rest?"

"Enter, Gaffer," said young Maria, "and seat ye here on the settle."

"Aye," said the little old man.

He seated himself before the hearth and stared at its gray ash solemnly as if a fire still burned there.

"Who might ye be, young lass?"

"Maria Hallettt of Eastham, sir."

"Would ye be knowing of a brave young sailorman, one who might desire a ship?" The old man glanced at the girl as he spoke and Maria, startled, became aware of the sharpening light in his eyes.

She stared at his cloak that hung to his knees, at his thin old hands, at his beady eyes, at his shoes that had never traversed the swamp, for the buckles shone like silver moons and never a trace of sand or marshwater clung to their smooth dark leather.

"Sir," she whispered in a choking voice, "sir, tell me who you are?"

The old man smiled. "A shipmaster, lass, one weary of the sea and gone too old for the bitter winds of voyaging. I've a trim little vessel, the sloop *Lilith,* and she sails out of Dartmouth Sea Gate. I be seeking a lad to gentle her now, one who will pay me a binder price and later share the lay."

"How many pieces of gold, sir, is the binder price for your ship?"

"Young Maria, I need no gold. The binder price is your note of hand."

"What will such a note say?"

"Five short words: FOR A SHIP A SOUL."

"What manner of talk is this, Gaffer?" Maria, Cape-canny and a reasoning lass, felt suddenly wroth and brave.

"Young ye be, oh, young and fair! Let pass an old man's folly."

The Old Comer stirred in his seat by the hearth then turned to face her squarely.

"Do ye love Sam Bellamy, heart and soul, as men say of ye in Tavern?"

"Aye, Gaffer, that I do."

"Then have ye given away your soul. And what have ye got in return for it? Possess ye Sam's completely?"

"Nay, Gaffer, a man's soul is never all of it given to a maid. Much of it goes to a ship."

"'Tis not given to man, 'tis not given to maid to possess a soul completely! Not your own soul, lass. Not that of your lover. Love's but its dragging anchor."

"Then how think you to purchase mine, Old Man, if I do not wholly possess it?"

"I desire only to secure some part of it, wrest it away from the quarrelsome Slave Masters — One in Heaven and One in Hell — who, without any right thereto, have indentured men's souls to Their service. Never shall I rest, nor ever die — since neither of These will let me in — till I possess such cargo of souls as will buy eternal freedom."

"I do not understand you, Gaffer."

"'Tis no matter, lass. My wits be dim. Their candles blow in a wandering wind. But harkee well: *For what soul may be yours, I offer a ship for your lover."*

"I take your offer," said Maria briskly. "I will give you my note of hand."

The old man rose from his seat by the hearth. He picked up the book on the table. "Let the note be writ here over your name." He returned the vellum book to her, with a hand wrinkled, thin-fingered and fine, so very transparent a hand that it might be the hand of a ghost.

Maria dipped the goose-quill pen in the clot of blood-soaked ash. Slowly she wrote over her name the words: FOR A SHIP A SOUL.

*   *   *

After supper in Hallett House, the Captain filled his pipe. He put on his buckskin Indian slippers and settled down by the fire. Maria, her soft skirts rustling, moved restlessly round the room. Now and again she looked intently at the darkness out of the window. The Captain watched her furtively, a frown between his eyes. She was all that mattered in the world to him; she was only a lass, and a scant fifteen, yet her life was going awry.

"Maria," said he gently, "come sit by the fire with me."

"I cannot, father. My heart turns within me."

"Is it about young Sam, Maria? What more could you ask than I have given? A mate's berth? A right to inherit? A good chance in the trade?"

"Father," said Maria suddenly, "will you take me tonight to Higgins Tavern? Will you let me talk to Sam? I desire to secure from him a promise of which you shall be a witness, sir — a pledge that he will not abandon your service to sign articles with the sea robbers."

"When a man's as sot as he be, Maria, argifying's no use."

"The gold of the Spanish galleon, father, like salt brine eats his soul. 'Tis the last night before you sail, and 'tis only I who can break Sam's will. Take me I pray to the Tavern."

Captain Hallett hedged. "Higgins Tavern by night," said he, "is no right place for a maid."

"I shall be safe if you take me, father. Summon Sam out to talk, if you will, down in the Apple Tree Hollow."

The Captain groaned. "Get your shawl," said he. "We'll stroll that way. 'Tis a longish path. Perchance I'll talk ye out of it."

In the warm summer night father and daughter walked through the pine-tree country till they saw the lights shining from the windows of the taproom of Higgins Tavern.

"I doubt the wisdom of this," said the Captain. "Do not forget I command the ship to which this boy is articled. He'll never meet up with the sea robbers, lass. If he holds to his course, thus grim of spirit, I'll clap him in irons; I'll lock him belowdecks whenever the ship makes port."

"This man is not dove nor sparrow, father. He is eagle born to soar. You cannot cage Sam Bellamy; he would die, prisoned in a ship."

As they approached the door of the Tavern, a hubbub of voices burst upon them.

"Turn ye back!" ordered the Captain promptly. "Turn ye back, Maria, *now!*"

"'Tis only roisterers," pleaded Maria. "The voices are happy, not angry. Let us learn what news is abroad."

Inside the taproom a crowd had assembled around a small table by the hearth. The room was dense with clay pipe smoke, and reeked with the indolent fumes of ale.

"'Tis a gambler's game. I will send for Sam."

Maria stood still in the doorway. "Father," she said, "it were wise if we learned what such uproar as this betides."

The Captain stood on a small stool to peer over the heads of the crowd.

"God A'mighty, 'tis Sam!" he exclaimed, "gambling with a little old man! There's a heap of gold coin beside the boy, enough to fill a swabber's bucket!"

Maria did not seem surprised.

A sudden hush came over the taverners through which like the ringing of a mellow bell, a fine old voice spoke clearly. "Young sailor, ye have won *all* my gold. Are ye ready for a last throw?"

"What have you left to wager, Gaffer?"

"The ship *Lilith*," said the little old man. "Here be her papers, out of Dartmouth. I am weary of the tricks of the sea, and I need my good gold back again. One more throw I offer ye, sailor. All of the gold ye have won tonight against the sloop *Lilith*."

Sam's eyes were blazing. "Done!" he cried. "Whatever she be, if ship can float."

"She's a slim, small craft," continued the gambler, "fitted for the Southern Seas."

He took the dice in his frail old hand and cast them out on the table. The tense watchers surged back as he threw, with exclamation and murmur. Sam gathered up the throw.

"Gaffer," he muttered, " 'tis folly, this, and passing strange in one of your years. Let us forsake such dangersome play. I'll give ye back your gold."

"Let be," said the old, old man to the boy. "I have had my day. What I do I do. If I lose this world's goods, mayhap at the last when I knock with my staff on Mother Earth, she will let me in to rest."

Sam cast the dice. A shout went up.

"The ship! Sam Bellamy has won a ship!"

"What ship is she?"

"The ship *Lilith!*"

"Never heerd tell of her!"

"What's her home port?"

"Sails out of Dartmouth."

"Let's see her papers!"

"Gold and a ship!"

"The boy's made a fortune."

In the doorway Maria swayed. She would have fallen, but her father caught her. "Hold to the door," he commanded sternly. "Have done with womanish foibles. I must go stop that blackhearted fool from cheating an old man."

He shouldered his way through the taproom, thrusting aside excited taverners who were passing the ship's papers from hand to hand, scrutinizing them eagerly, till their heads nigh knocked together.

"Sam," cried the Captain, "I'm shamed for ye, boy. Give back this man his papers."

"I like it not overly much myself." Sam spoke gravely, slowly.

Old Captain Howes was holding the port papers close to his long red nose. He spoke in a high and querulous voice: "Man and boy for fifty year I've sailed out of Dartmouth Sea Gate. I be knowing her ships," said he, "all ships that claim the port. Never heerd of the sloop *Lilith*. These papers I say be false."

Captain Hallett turned to make inquiry of the old gaffer at the table, but the gambler's seat was empty.

"Where's the ship's owner?" demanded the Captain.

"He took himself off."

"Where to? Where to?"

The onlookers took up the cry: "Where's the ship's owner?

"Where's the old man?"

Three of the taverners hurried outside. They called lustily into the night but their voices echoed in mocking return. And all the while Sam stood very still like one gone suddenly daft, staring, staring blankly at the papers thrust back in his hand.

"*Lilith*," he murmured, "the ship *Lilith!* I must give her back — yet I won her fairly. 'Tis asking much, to give up a ship! I could give up gold, or a woman, or a crown, but a ship I cannot forswear."

They searched for the old man high and low, fearful that he had done himself in. They took lanterns and searched through the Burying Acre and down in the Apple Tree Hollow. Then Long John the Indian and the younger goodmen ranged through the pine-tree country and over the nearer dunes. But the Old Comer had disappeared, leaving no tracks in the dune-sand, no mark on the needles of the pine country. When the searchers gathered again in the taproom for a nightcap and a final recounting, they surmised that he must have drowned himself in the waters of the Minister's Pond.

At the height of the search, Captain Hallett, directing it, stepped out the tavern door. Then Maria passed quickly through the smoke-filled room till she stood before Sam Bellamy.

"Sam," she said, "you have won a ship."

"Aye, Maria, but I cannot believe that this strange

vessel is mine. This very night I set forth for Dartmouth. If I come not back, you will know, my darling, that the sloop *Lilith* is seaworthy craft and that I have sailed her to the Spanish Indies to raise the sunken treasure."

"And then, Sam?"

"Why then, Maria, I shall return," vowed young Samuel Bellamy, "return to wed you with book and ring on the decks of a tall three-master. Return to carry you far away from this wilderness town on the Great Sea Hook. I shall dress you in damask and satin and pearls. You shall go in a coach to the English Court. You shall make your bow at the Ivory Throne. You shall dance at the Court of Spain."

"If you will wed me," said Maria Hallett, "wed me fairly by book and ring, and mayhap buy me a silken shawl, 'tis as much as I dare to hope."

"You sound," said Sam sourly, "just like your Aunt Samantha."

"She is kin to me," responded wryly the Cape Cod sea trader's daughter. And she smiled her new little crooked smile while Captain Hallett, returning to the taproom, put her bright shawl about her shoulders and led his pale and lovely daughter out through the tavern door.

3

The Stoning of Maria

T HE WINTER of 1706 was a terrible time for Eastham. In the autumn the crops failed, and by spring there was famine in the village. During the stormy month of February great gales lashed the coast. In one of these the *Flower of the Horn* was overset and sank. Captain Hallett perished and with him were drowned six of the strong, young Eastham boys whom he had taken on as crew.

During Christmas week Abigail was married to Captain Caleb Snow. She left Hallett House on New Year's Day for a small new home built by her husband far out in the Dune Country, not very far from the

39

treacherous swamp that surrounded Doane Island.

Aunt Samantha objected: "'Tis out of village. 'Tis too nigh to the sea. The waters will talk a body deef. 'Tis only temptation to thieving piratemen. What's more, 'tis no safe place for babes!"

But Abigail and her young captain had "quare, new-fangled notions." They desired to behold through glass windows long stretches of the bluewater. Also, since the Dune Country belonged by right to Snows, there the young couple might have their land free save for the cost of the transfer papers. And Abigail who was thrifty realized how much her husband longed to exchange his old ship for a new one. She settled the matter firmly. "I shall be happy only there, where the seas over which my husband sails behold me of a stormy night entreating God for his safety."

In March Captain Snow set forth for the spring voyage to the Indies. He begged Maria and Aunt Samantha to stay in the new house by the dunes with Abigail who was with child. "Bring her back to the village," said Samantha firmly. "Bring her back to Hallett House where she belongs." So Abigail returned in the spring to her old home in the South Parish and was startled to find how much Maria had changed in a brief winter, changed from a young, tumultuous child to a grave and silent woman.

The village commented freely on the difference in Maria's ways. The story of the gamble for the ship

Lilith, repeated over and over again, grew in the re-telling. And after the loss of the *Flower of the Horn* with the death of Captain Hallett and his fine young Eastham crew, townspeople looked askance at Maria, and she gave up going to village chatterfests, making excuse of a winter cough and later that Abigail needed her.

In April the Reverend Mr. Samuel Treat, Minister of the South Parish, rode over to Hallett House. He talked for a while with Aunt Samantha, then summoned Maria down from her room to which she had retreated in a hurry when she saw the Minister coming.

"Maria," began the Parson, "you're the smartest lass I know. What's come over ye? Is it true you are lovelorn and plighted to the English sailor who won a ship by gambling?"

"Aye," said Maria. "I love Sam Bellamy, and when he returns from the West Indies, we twain shall marry."

"Sam Bellamy is a godless man. You had best forget him."

"Parson, you would not ask of me that if you knew how matters were."

By the tight look of Maria's face old Mr. Treat saw that he might do a woeful harm to her if he did not leave her soul be. So he nodded and put his hand on her head. "God be with you, Maria," he prayed. "I'll do what I can to quiet town's talk, but if you would make a home for Sam Bellamy, here in Eastham Parish, then you must help me to lay the gossip and come to church of a Sunday."

Maria drew away from him. "Parson," she answered, "to my lips no longer rise the dutiful words of obedience and prayer. In my heart no longer bides the meek submission, the grateful love required by Holy Book."

"What mean you, child?"

"Parson! Parson!" Into Maria's young voice crept a note of sharp despair. "I am afraid to cross the doorstone of the Holy House of God! Lest I be turned to an old hag, as I have heerd tell happens to those who have stood against the Lord!"

Samuel Treat shivered. He drew his worn Indian shawl about his weary shoulders. Woven for him by the loving hands of his loyal Indian converts, its touch brought comfort and reassurance when he felt as now that he failed of his calling — to save all souls in his parish.

"God forgive you, Maria," said he. "You know not the terrible thing you say. Come hither to me, my daughter. Say for me the Lord's Prayer."

Maria's face childlike and fair was as white as the Cape seaflower. "And if I cannot, Parson?"

"Then of a truth you have been bewitched, but of that I have scant belief."

Maria folded her small hands together. In a clear passionless voice she repeated: "Our father, which art in Heaven, hallowed be Thy name . . ."

The minister drew a sigh of relief. "Maria! Maria!" he exclaimed thankfully. "You are *not* beleaguered of the Devil!"

"Think you 'tis simple as that, Parson? What the tongue says is matter of habit and easily shaped to the asking; but the heart lies hid in the breast."

Old Mr. Treat left Hallett House with a vague disquiet in his mind. He tried to argue that Maria Hallet was a child bereaved and grieving, that continued addiction to book learning bemused the female mind. To him she seemed too young and fair to have need of the wiles of witchery — more often an answer to an old maid's plight, or a goodwife's haven in a storm. He comforted himself with the recollection of her clear and gentle voice repeating the words of the sacred prayer.

Spring that brought with it famine brought also a pestilence to the cattle. Calves died as they dropped. Cows sickened and failed to give milk, and the muttering that had been behind closed doors in the winter was spoken aloud on the sandy streets of the troubled town of Eastham.

"'Tis bewitchment upon us!"

"'Tis the work of the Devil!"

"Who has brought us such woes and disasters?"

"Ah — I could tell ye!" — with a shrug of the shoulders! And before the half sentences were completed, the name of Maria Hallett was on the goodwives' lips.

In late May, Long John the Coast Watcher brought news that Captain Snow's ship had been sighted on the southern seaway. Abigail was filled with excitement and joyful plans for his home-coming. Maria went shopping in the village with a large market basket and before she had halfway filled it up with Aunt Samantha's needments, she began to be sorry that she had not ridden her father's mare to town.

For herself she made two purchases, a small leaflet on the India trade and a pair of long bone needles to fashion a cloak and bonnet for Abigail's expected baby. She stuck the needles, protruding upward, into the rim of the basket. She tucked the pamphlet about the Indies into the pocket of her skirt. Then carrying the loaded basket at her side, and with frequent pauses for handshifts, Maria started down the King's Highway past Eastham South Parish Church.

The church had a small slope of "cover ground" brought by sea from Boston. This rich loam, tended by the deacons, grew very green with grass, and here and there along its edges blossomed a flowering bush. Suddenly between two of these a small child chased by a larger ran into the sand of the roadway, and tripped by the sudden drag on his feet, he pitched head-first on the basket. The long bone needle that protruded upward entered the child's eye. Screaming with terror he fell to the ground, as blood gushed from the wound. Maria dropped the basket. She seized the terrified child in her arms, and hurried to the Parsonage door.

"Parson, Parson!" she called frantically, pounding with the heavy door knocker.

The door was opened by Sylvester Treat, the Parson's youngest son. "Father is gone parish visiting," said he. "You must not enter here, Mistress Hallett. Begone, O wicked witch!"

Maria brushed the boy aside. She deposited the screaming child on the wide settle in the greatroom. Hurrying into the summer kitchen, she soaked a towel in a bucket of water, wiped off the blood as best she could, then taking another clean towel, she bandaged the small head.

The child had lost consciousness and lay in a stiff-bodied faint.

"Sylvester," said Maria sternly, "go summon Mehitabel Tucker and then run for the doctor."

Sylvester hurried up the street to Mehitabel Tucker's door. Mehitabel was a midwife and an excellent hand at doctoring. She gathered together a few necessaries and ran down the road to the Parsonage while Sylvester raced toward the doctor's house which stood at the end of the street.

The doctor was tending ride-away patients. Sylvester left him some startling news, then swaggered back along the King's Highway, greeted by questioning goodwives, by curious gaffers, by wide-eyed children

who had heard the child's frantic screams. Sylvester
found this audience greatly to his taste. He trumpeted
forth a shocking account of the events of the morning
till like the Pied Piper he gathered around him a group
of credulous followers who trooped after him down
the road and through the parsonage door. On the
threshold of the greatroom he stopped and pointed a
begrimed finger at Maria who knelt by the settle.

"That's her! That's the witch woman there. She put
her finger on Andrew's eye. She killed him with one
touch. I seen her do it," said Sylvester Treat enlarg-
ing on his scanty evidence, "out of the bedroom window."

"Will he live?" asked Maria in an anguish of fear,
her eyes on Mistress Tucker's face.

"I have hope of it," answered the midwife gravely.

Then Maria, who had been too absorbed to hear
Sylvester's words, felt a firm hand on her shoulder, and
the kind, wise wife of Israel Howes spoke in her quiet
manner.

"Maria," she said, "you must not stay here. I will
take your place and help Mehitabel. You will only
bring about new disasters. Mayhap harm will befall
you."

Maria looked up perplexed and dazed.

"There was no one to see," explained Mistress
Howes, "what chanced betwixt you and this boy. 'Tis
better for you, better for the child, better for us all if

you hasten home. Let Mehitabel, myself and the doctor care for what damage has been done."

Maria turned and gazed steadily at the goodwives in the doorway. Ashamed, their glances shifted furtively from her tense and sorrowful face. Then she rose from her knees, and groped her way blindly, fumblingly out of the room. The goodwives shrank away from her path as she stumbled out the door and down the path, till by chance she came to the market basket that still stood beside a blood-spotted patch of sand on the edge of the King's Highway. Lifting the basket in her two hands, she staggered down the road till she turned into the pine-tree path out of sight of watching eyes.

Abigail was alarmed by Maria's long delay in the village. Fearful that the laden basket had proved too heavy a burden, she stared anxiously out the window. When at last Maria appeared, Abigail was shocked to see the dragging footsteps, the bent shoulders of her blithe young cousin. She rushed out of the door.

"Maria, what is it? Are you hurt? Are you ill?"

"No, Abigail, only spent."

Maria put the basket on the kitchen table. Avoiding Abigail's keen blue eyes, she climbed the stairs, went into her bedroom and bolted the bedroom door.

Within a week a festering destroyed the boy's damaged eye. A fortnight later Andrew Nickerson, aged four, kissed the Bible, spake the Lord's Prayer, com-

mended his parents to the care of the angels and went
to join his God. When Maria Hallett heard this news,
against the wishes of Aunt Samantha she walked down
to the village to carry to Andrew Nickerson's mother
fifty pieces of gold. That was a very great gift for
those sparse times in the Colony, but Maria knew that
the family were poor and the gold would provide many
comforts and needments for Andrew's brothers and sisters.

Abigail pleaded in vain with Maria to wait for one
more day, wait until Captain Snow returned from the
Province Lands where he had gone to attend to the
lading of his ship. At nightfall he would be back in
Eastham, and the next day might accompany Maria to
Andrew Nickerson's house. But Maria could not wait.
Filled with forebodings and self-reproach she desired
more than aught else in the world to gaze on little
Andrew's face and give her gift to his mother.

Abigail insisted on going, so the two set forth together. When they approached the Nickerson house
they saw, to Abigail's swift misgiving, that a dozen
women had assembled outside it and were talking in
low tones.

"There she is now!" cried an angry voice.

"Look on her, in her fine clothes with her fancy
ways!"

"What do you here, witch woman?"

"How fares your lover in his Devil Ship?"

"Have you not brought enough suffering to East-ham Parish ere this?"

"I have come," said Maria, "to share the gold that my father left me with these good people for whose affliction I am much to blame, and whose sorrow I long to ease."

One of the women laughed shrilly. "Tainted gold!" she screamed hysterically. "Touch it not! Turn the witch from the door!"

"The Devil's Pence is in her hand! The Devil's Honey on her tongue!"

The group of women drew nearer together and closer to the doorstone.

"Maria," said Abigail gently, "'tis best that we go home. This can be done another day after Parson Treat has talked to these goodwives and lifted them out of their folly."

Maria stood still and straight. "I shall not turn and fly from these," she answered in cold clear tones. "I shall enter this house of sorrow, to bring what I have to those who may need it in this most grievous trouble." She advanced toward the group at the door.

Suddenly one of the women reached down and plucked up a small stone from a pile that the children of the house had gathered together to edge a posy bed. The stone went wild. Maria continued to walk toward the muttering group. Panic seized on the goodwives as she gazed on them with stern eyes.

"She's putting the Evil Eye on us!"

"Remember the *Flower of the Horn!*"

"She drowned her father and the Eastham boys!"

More hands reached for stones. Swiftly Abigail stepped forward between Maria and the goodwives. "I offer my body," said Abigail Snow, "and that of my unborn child, to prove to you that of my true knowledge Maria Hallett is no witch. These deaths I swear were not of her doing. She has practised no evil magic."

A stone struck Abigail on the breast, and as Maria in turn tried to screen her, a stone struck Maria on the temple and she sank, swaying, to the ground. Abigail knelt over her. She was already big with child, and seeing her thus, some sense of what they had done came to the women of Eastham Parish. Shamefaced, they withheld their stoning. Slowly they withdrew to the little house and closed and barred its door.

Maria lay as one dead on the path. Abigail sobbed beside her. There Samuel Treat came upon the two girls, having had word of their stoning. He raised Abigail to her feet. He chafed Maria's hands. Soon she opened her sea-blue eyes and murmured, "Father, father."

"Maria," said the old Parson as he stroked back the hair from her bruised forehead, "what has overtaken ye?"

She sat up dizzily. Then memory returned. "Where are they?" she asked numbly. "They stoned me, and they stoned Abigail. Mayhap I am a witch, Parson, but the stone that was meant to destroy my powers struck Abigail on the breast! And whether the Devil take me or leave me, Abigail was born of the angels. *She has never sinned.*"

Samuel Treat led the two girls down a strangely deserted road and into the Parsonage door. He gave them each a cup of wine and bade them rest in the best poster bed until after the night had fallen. For Sylvester he cut a sizable switch and the boy and his father retired promptly behind the door of the woodshed.

After darkness Samuel Treat accompanied the cousins to Hallett House. Abigail wondered whether it was of neglect or of intention that he took no lantern to light their path through the shadowy pine-tree country.

When Aunt Samantha heard what had happened, her bonnet went awry. Her black eyes blazed and she shook her fists as she paced the greatroom, back and forth. There were seamen's words on her lips.

Late that night Captain Snow arrived. He was met at the door of Hallett House by the Reverend Mr. Samuel Treat who had decided to remain in the house until the Captain's return.

Abigail had been put to bed. She was dizzy, her head throbbing. Her breast where the stone had hit her swelled and the swelling pained severely. Long John was sent for the doctor.

Then young Captain Snow and Samantha Doane and the Reverend Mr. Samuel Treat entered the front parlor. There, with the door discreetly closed, they remained for a long time. When the Minister took his leave at last, Captain Snow, and Maria who had a heavy bruise over the right temple but otherwise showed no ill effects from her stoning, sat down at table with Aunt Samantha and they tried to eat, though appetite failed them, the long-delayed home-coming meal.

It had been agreed that all four must leave Hallett House and live for a time in the house that Captain Snow had built for his bride in the Dune Country. After supper Maria and Samantha set about a night of packing. An hour before Sun-coming Captain Snow walked into Eastham village. There he procured a post horse and returned at First-hour-light. In the morning Long John arrived with the doctor, and with an Indian pony. The doctor dressed Abigail's breast. He shook his head in anxiety; yet he too advised that the little family leave Eastham Parish and live for a while in the Dune Lands to seaward. He faithfully promised Caleb Snow that at least once a week he would ride over-dune to visit Abigail until her wound was healed.

She was dressed by Aunt Samantha, and lifted to the back of Captain Hallett's mare who was gentle and placid, knew the girls well, and turned her head and whinnied, as if she also understood that things were not as they should be.

Maria closed the great front door, then turned and looked back at the stately house in which she had been born. "For the first time since thou wert built," she

said, using the Old Comer words, "thy friendly hearth
grows cold."

She climbed on the back of Long John's pony and
Samantha mounted the post horse. Chests were
strapped to the saddles. The young captain and the
tall silent Indian accompanied this small calvalcade
on foot. Captain Snow carried a pistol; Long John, his
gun.

Abigail swayed in the saddle. Her husband held
her with one strong arm and Long John walked, holding the bridle, on the other side of the horse. Aunt
Samantha followed. Maria led the way.

The June day was misty and cool. When at last they
reached the Dune Country, its sands were swathed in a
delicate fog, and Abigail's house in the drifting mist
looked like a house in a dream.

Long John entered first. He lit the fire piled high
with logs and the glow of it shone with a comforting
warmth through the mist-beaded, small-paned windows.

"We are home at last," sighed Abigail.

Captain Snow carried her up the narrow seashell
path and across the doorstone. He laid her on the bed
in the upstep bedroom and hoisted Maria's and
Samantha's chests upladder to the sleeproom in the loft.
Samantha undressed Abigail, who shivered though the
bed was carefully warmed with stones heated in the
fire. Caleb Snow opened a bottle of red Madeira wine
and Maria cooked up a posset. Abigail sipping a cup

of this was soon warm again and smiling. She explained the ways of the little house with a housewife's eager pride.

In a week's time the wound on her breast grew better. The doctor ceased to urge caution and the application of hot poultices swathed in oven-baked linen. He joked with the young wife. Slowly also Maria regained some of her old interests. On sunny mornings she would walk out to stand on the Dune Before the Sea and gaze long at the green reefwater and the ships that traversed the seaway. Sometimes on a golden afternoon she would pick her way along the hidden marsh path, wade through the shadowy green pool and arrive at the Secret Island that had belonged to her forebears and to which they too retreated for a space in their hours of doubt and peril.

Once on a blue moonlight night as she was walking over the dunes, she saw silhouetted against starred skies a strange little figure with a feather in its cap, standing on the crest of a dune.

" 'Tis daft ye be," said Abigail, "moonstruck and love-lorn." The two girls laughed. Almost it seemed that the terrible memories of the village stoning were being thrust aside.

But Aunt Samantha treated news of this small figure in a different way. "Dobbies!" she exclaimed. " 'Tis a parlous error to let them into the Colony. Now there'll be raids on the larder! There'll be night riding of the mare. Flimsy of wit and cocking her neck *she*'ll soon fall under their blandishments. Saint

Godric's stone will save us."

The day following Maria's report Samantha walked along the dunes till she came on a path that led down to the beach. There, after some searching, she found a stone with a hole in the center of it. This she brought back in her pocket.

"Saint Godric's stone," said she firmly, "must be hung over the shed. Dobby folk be pestersome imps even in the Old Country. What they'll be up to of wildness and folly, far away in this wilderness land, I dare not put my mind to!"

As the days passed Abigail's thoughts centered on the child who was to come and on her husband who might be expected to return from his voyage by mid-Autumn. She was fearful lest the child be born before Caleb's return. Her breast, though she spoke no word of it, had grown stiff and hard in the sensitive place where the heavy bruise had been. It pained at night and throbbed to the touch when she put her finger upon it.

In mid-October the Captain returned and a week later Abigail Snow gave birth to a son who was named Jeremy after the Captain's father. The doctor who rode over from Eastham arrived after the birth. But Maria and Aunt Samantha, wise as Cape women were wont to be in the days when doctors were seldom available, delivered the child well. The tiny boy was spanked, washed and laid in his wooden cradle. But a terrible festering had broken out in Abigail's wounded breast. She was unable to nurse the child so Maria was given the task of mixing a few drops of Jamaica rum with warmed cow's milk. This young Jeremy sucked from her finger and seemed to like it well.

Two weeks after the birth of her son Abigail Snow died. Toward the end when she knew that she must go, she summoned Maria to her bedside and stroking the shining corn-colored hair she spoke gently of the past.

"I have loved you well, Maria," said she, "but I know that I am dying. There is none in the world who will care as you for little Jeremy, my son. Could you perhaps find it in your heart some day to take my place?"

Maria's pulse beat wildly. She desired to say yea to Abigail, but the strange, dark, wide-browed face of Sam Bellamy rose before her eyes.

"Abigail," she said softly, "we have been close since we were young. Let me be free, but this I promise. Whatever I can, I shall do for your son. Whatever he needs, if it be in my power, that I shall secure for him, even at price of my life. Now I am blackened as a witch woman. It will be well, for a time at least, if I stay clear of his loving."

"Hush," said Abigail, "hush, Maria. You are no witch. Have you not slept in my arms of a night with the peace of the stars shining down on us?"

Tears poured down Maria's cheeks. "Abigail, Abigail," she sobbed and laid her head on the counterpane and the gentle hand stroked her hair until at last it was still.

The day that Abigail Snow died Maria went to the Secret Island. For long hours she sat alone in the little hut around which stood a crumbling wooden stockade. When she returned, the moon was high, candles were lit in the little house, and watchers sat by the bed of Abigail who looked in her hour of isolate peace calm and unafraid.

Maria knelt beside the cradle of the tiny sleeping child. "Jeremy," she said, "little Jeremy, it were best that I leave you." And after the funeral she made known to Aunt Samantha and Captain Snow her intention of selling Hallett House and rebuilding with the aid of Long John the hut on the Secret Island. Unexpectedly Aunt Samantha did not oppose this plan. She was preoccupied with the child, who had lost weight and was not thriving.

Samuel Treat rode out to the Dune Lands to advise against Maria's decision. But Long John, who had curious powers of persuasion over the Minister, spoke with him at length in the Indian language and opposition ceased.

With the boards of the old stockade Long John and Captain Snow repaired and rebuilt the Island hut. They brought by horse from Hallett House the few belongings that Maria requested. They placed these in the tiny home, and it was mid-December before the house was completed. One cold, raw, windy morning Maria wrapped round her the scarlet shawl, last gift from her father, and mounted an Indian pony. Accompanied by Long John on foot, who carried strapped to his back the jeweled chest covered with sailcloth, she ventured out on the sand bar that led into the Golden Marsh. The out tides had lowered the pool and without wetting the scarlet shawl which, to Aunt Samantha's amazement and perplexity, she had chosen to wear for this journey, Maria stepped over the doorstone of the tiny house hidden in the center of the dark pine-tree island.

Captain Snow had done what he could to make the house less lonely. A bright fire burned on the hearth. The larder was well stocked with food. There were new stout bars on the windows. And a tiny blue-eyed kitten sprawled on the settle beside the fire. Maria gazed at this furry mite. She picked it up tenderly in her two hands and gave it back to the Captain.

" 'Twould never do, Caleb," said she, "for a witch woman to own a cat. If the goodwives of Eastham got word of this they would set fire to the Island."

The kitten wailed. The Captain's face grew stern with protest and sorrow. "Maria," he said, "you are no witch. 'Tis false reasoning, 'tis wild tarradiddles befog the goodwives' wits. Why must you live in this lonely fashion which will make tongues wag the faster? Come back with me to the Dune Country. The boy Jeremy needs you. There will be nothing young in his life when I am gone to sea."

Maria took off her scarlet shawl and seated herself on the settle. "Here I belong, and here I bide." Light from the fire woke in the shawl a pattern of waxing and waning moons broidered in a gold thread.

4

The House on the
Secret Island

In the spring of the year 1708 Maria heard a small cry in the night outside her bedroom window, the cry of an injured animal, like the whimper of a small dog. She took a storm lantern in her hand, wrapped her dark cloak about her, and went out into the night. The whimpering grew louder and she found on the edge of the pine-tree forest a wolf cub with its leg broken. Maria gathered it into her arms, made a splint for the broken paw, and laid the small, emaciated body in a nest of cloth by the fire.

That same week word came through that Sam Bellamy had gone on the account. For a long year in the hot Indies he had toiled over a water-logged wreck and spent his last farthing, with never sixpence to show for it, not to mention silver or gold. The sloop *Lilith*, in the last days of the desperate, futile treasure-raising, had her hull stove in on a reef. She was patched by Sam with a masterly skill but the wise old salts kept clear of her.

With Sam worked a Nantucket sailorman named Paul Williams and the two became close friends. When Sam decided to turn pirate, Paul Williams put in with him, so the two alone, lacking wages for a crew, sailed the sloop *Lilith* about the Southern Seas, seeking for a pirate fleet. They fell in at last with Benjamin Horneygold, a stouthearted buccaneer in command of the ship *Mary Ann*. With him the two would-be pirates signed articles for a year, and the *Lilith* a shattered derelict, was left to drift like a ghost vessel toward the Sargasso Sea.

When news of Sam's piratical ventures began to reach Cape Cod, Maria sent Long John to the tavern to get direct word from the southern captains.

" 'Tis true," he said. "They say in tavern this Spawn of Lucifer has turned pirate. Soon he will murder the innocent. You must forget him now."

That night Maria opened the chest. For long hours she pored over the vellum-bound books from within it. Sun-coming was nigh when she heard a knock, a gentle, hesitant, memorable knock at the door of her island home. Maria unbarred the door.

"Enter, Old Comer," said she kindly. " 'Tis a strange hour for one of your age to venture through a wilderness swamp."

"I could not sleep for remembrance," said the Old Comer moodily, as he seated himself on the settle by the fire.

"Fair was the bargain, fair ye kept it, but a just due ye have not had from it — though life's like that, young lass. A man seldom gets what he bargains for."

"Yet," said Maria, child of her time, "whatever betide, so long as he may, a man must abide by his bargain."

"Aye, 'tis the rule of the Colonies, but 'tis not so in the China Seas where if fortune destroy a deal's intent, neither party be bound to the bargain. Nor is it true of the Holy Book writ in an Eastern tongue. Nor of One in Heaven — nor One in Hell. Smooth and clear be *their* sailing orders, yet they turn from the wheel in the hour of the storm and let the brave ships founder."

"I have not complained," said Maria Hallett.

"I like ye for it well."

"But 'tis true," said the sea trader's daughter, "that I have now more need of a soul than I have of a masterless vessel."

"And I have need of more souls than one, so I offer ye fair bargain: *For the soul's return, a ship, Maria* — for the soul's return, a ship!"

"But I have no ship to trade you, Gaffer. The sloop

Lilith, so mariners say, drifts derelict in Deadmen's Sea."

"Have ye not books for the learning of Spells?"

"Aye, Gaffer, in the jeweled chest lies the Wisdom of the Ages."

"What would ye do with this knowledge, lass?"

" 'Tis a trust I hold for the sons of men."

"If ye die, whence goes the chest?"

"To a boy who lives over-dune, Gaffer. One whose mother was pure of heart, whose father is a brave captain. The boy I will trust when the time comes for it. He will not betray me."

"Ye are of womanish mind, Maria. Ye trust too much to the sons of men."

"I but guard with my life the books, Gaffer, lest their terrible power be put to wrong use. How this power will fare in after time I have no means of knowing."

"Power is but a wheel's turning, lass, as every helmsman knows. It lies dark at the center of the wheel which turns now up and it turns now down, and for him who rises one shall fall. Evil and good are inseparable."

"I do not believe you, Gaffer. But if you have bargain to make with me, I will hear its terms right gladly."

"I am old, lass; my hands unsteady. I dare not practice alchemies. But there is a vial, a magic potion, hid under the chest's till, and there is a book of moons and tides. Concealed it be by a hidden panel under yon wooden lid.

"'Tis an ancient brew the vial holds, a potion made from a mooncast — from the shed skin of the snake Lilith, the golden snake that coiling sways in the black tree of heaven." The old man nodded as if drifting toward sleep, then stirred and muttered softly: "Again from the sky her mooncast falls, as once it fell on a Grecian hill, and in a golden haze lies floating over this wilderness marsh."

Maria went to the cupboard and poured for him a glass of wine. While he drank this, she opened the chest and found that the lining at the bottom of the till could be lifted out revealing a recess in which was secured a tiny, sealed vial. With her delicate fingers she felt along the wood of the lid's panel. It yielded at length and from it fell a small blacklettered book.

With the book and the vial she returned to the settle. The Old Comer roused. His eyes brightened.

"For these twain," said Maria Hallett, "will you give me my lost soul back?"

"Nay, lass, your soul comes high. By the words of the book compound ye potions to master the tides and the winds at sea. And when ye have sunk me a fine ship, with a cargo of souls for the using, then shall ye have your one soul back. 'Tis a trick ye soon can master."

"I shall not drown young sailors, Gaffer, for the sake of my own soul's saving."

"As ye will, lass. The dawn has come. And I must traverse the mooncast now back to town and tavern. But I see in your eyes the folly that fills ye, as it fills all this wilderness land with a restless, cruel striving — the faith that with power ye will overthrow evil — power in the wheel's turning."

"Gaffer, if this book teaches me how to quiet the storm-tossed waves of the sea, what sin could there be in that?"

"Gentle the waves as ye will, lass, but there'll come a time, if ye master the tides, when the seas will *rise* at your bidding. Then plight me a ship for the soul's return. The offer bides, Maria."

*   *   *

In time the story of Maria Hallett, living alone on the Secret Island, reached the Province Lands. Devil-may-care sailors of the port drank to her health in tavern and boasted of schemes to risk their lives for her father's gold and her beauty. The tale grew apace. The boasts increased. At last two young and braggardy boys determined to venture on a moonlit night into the Golden Swamp. Armed with cutlasses and pistols, they set forth for the Island. One had been trained as an Indian tracker, so in time they found the short strip of bar that pierced the narrow inlet. They traveled the bar some hundreds of feet before they failed of a turning. Then one was drawn down like a plummeting stone. The other tried to save his fellow and screamed aloud for help.

Maria heard the cries. She came out of her house, with a lantern and a rope. By her side walked the young wolf.

"Where away?" she called in answer to the frantic cries and oaths. But before she could wade the Green Pool, the cries lapsed in a sudden silence. And though twice she traveled the hidden path, no one was there to bespeak her. Only the wolf paused at a place some hundreds of feet from the shoreline. There Maria lowered her lantern and saw how the sands were scuffed.

That night a fire burned till dawn on the hearth of the island house. Maria concocted a strange brew. She muttered words in the Latin tongue. At dawn she carried the brew outside and poured it into the marsh.

Thereafter it was said in tavern that Maria was in league with pirates, that sea marauders had found a haven and buried their treasure in her wood.

At night lanterns shone in the treachery swamp and there were men's voices talking together and the sounds of reckless brawling. Now and again covetous dreamers with a yearning for adventure approached the Golden Marsh. They were greeted by angry guttural voices, by cries and shouts, by threats and laughter. So they went back to the Province Lands and told what they had heard.

Between the years 1708 and 1717 miraculous good fortune seemed to follow all Cape ships. They ventured for trade round the Horn to China, and up the Indian Ocean. In the winter months of heavy storms there were few maritime losses. Sometimes it seemed as if Cape vessels were a special concern of the heavenly hosts, and as a result, a great reputation came to the Cape Cod captains. They were acknowledged by the whole wide world to be the most daring of navigators, and the shrewdest traders in the ports.

Captain Snow bought a new vessel, the ship of which Abigail dreamed. The sloop was named for his dead wife and proved swift-footed and quick to respond to the young captain's mastery. Men came to believe that Caleb Snow was the wisest mariner of the northern coasts for in some strange way when other ships lagged or were delayed by fog or storm, over the *Abigail* breezes moved, or the clouds parted and the fogs lifted. Even the angry winter seas seemed to buffet her less heavily than ships of a greater burden.

Now and again word was passed of Horneygold and Bellamy. They too prospered and with Captain Leboues, French Huguenot from Rochelle, at first they made rich captures in the Indies, but after a time the takes diminished, for Horneygold refused to plunder English vessels, and Spanish ships were fast disappearing from the routes of the old Armadas. In the weeks and months when the pirate fleet lay anchored

in hidden harbors Sam saw a chance to foster disaffec-
tion among the idle crews. When the matter of plun-
dering English ships was finally put to the vote, only
twenty-six pirates agreed to follow Horneygold. Ninety
elected Sam Bellamy as their new captain.

So Bellamy, Williams and Leboues sailed the seas
in concert, and though they sank no English ships, they
took a number of these as prizes and released captive
crews on shore. Unlike the other privateersmen and
buccaneers of the Indies, they kept no Glory Holes for
treasure but carried their riches in the holds of their
ships, keeping close contact together.

Maria grew from a fair young maid into a beautiful
woman. Oft in the night as she sat by her fire she
would cast a drop from a vial in her hand into the
rising flame. Clear shone the blaze, like a shining
mirror, and Maria was wont to watch therein the great
ships sailing their courses. Whether or not hers was
the power that brought them safe to harbor, in those
first decades of the eighteenth century the daring
prowess, the widening trade routes, the glorious cargoes from the Eastern voyages, brought to the young
maritime colony dreams of a vast trade empire built
by her gallant conquerors of wind and tide and
star.

*   *   *

In the year 1717, on a night when the moon was full

in April, Maria sat by her hearthstone. The lame wolf who had grown half blind lay gazing with yellow vacant eyes at the uprising fire.

"Wu Wang," said Maria, "we have disproved the Old Comer's evil warning. Power we have used for the welfare of men. Knowledge is kin to virtue."

The wolf cocked pointed ears. A sound of scratching echoed against the barred door of the greatroom.

"Who waits without?" called Maria.

No answer came, but again sounded a small importunate scratching low on the barred door.

"Who is there? Who is without?" cried Maria, perplexed and uneasy.

"Who? Who?" echoed an owl perched high on the rooftree.

Slowly Maria opened the door. The light from a pine torch burning on the table fell upon a small white dog standing alone on the doorstone, a bedraggled dog of a kind that Maria had never seen in the Colony. His fur was wet. Blood from his paw dripped red on the gray stone. And he gazed at Maria Hallett with the most urgent and beseeching look that she had ever beheld.

The Book
of
Bimini

An Interlude
in the Mooncast

1

The Dune People

JEREMY lifted the lid off the basket. In it crouched a dog. It blinked in the light; pricked its ears. Its nostrils twitched to the smell of wild turkey roasting on the open hearth. It tried to dig its paws into the bottom of the basket, to brace its small, bruised body against uncertain fate.

Three pairs of bright eyes stared down upon the dog. "Bah!" said the owner of the black eyes. "Is it your notion, Caleb, that this pocket-kerchief pup will protect us from bad Indians, or piratemen, or thieves?"

"He's a Scots Highlander," answered the tall man in whose eyes bantering humor lurked like the sun down-slanting on tidewater. "And the dog will grow, Samantha — though never very big. But he has the heart of a young lion and he'll brave death for his master."

"Who might that master be, Caleb?"

"The boy is to be his master, Samantha. 'Tis time Jeremy had body of life beholden to his governance."

The owner of the shining eyes drew closer to the basket. He spoke for the first time.

"What is the dog's name, father?"

"He goes by the name of Bimini."

For a moment Bimini laid his snout down on his trembling paws. He crouched low, flattened his ears. The basket in which he had been imprisoned had been lashed to the back of the Captain's saddle for many hours of riding. He was bruised and shaken; his thick white coat felt matted. He remained down-crouched while all around him eddied the scent of human kind, centered on him, broken by sounds: the hiss and sputter of a hearth fire, the tenes breathing of the boy.

Then he stood up unsteadily, put one paw on the basket's rim and slowly, fearfully, cautiously, he looked into Jeremy's face.

"Hi, Bimini!" said Jeremy. He lifted the pup and held him close. "Ye be far littler than I," he whispered "but we be two together. Two to keep sea watch over the dunes! Two to fight off the sea robbers!"

Bimini barked softly. He wriggled a little, put up his head and licked Jeremy's nose.

Three weeks after Bimini's arrival a big sea chest was brought into the greatroom and filled with sailorman's clothes. Into it went a compass in a box and a brace of shining pistols, a roll of charts and a rum-soaked spice cake, a Bible and a gold button coat.

In midafternoon Long John brought his Indian pony, Seesaw, to the door. The chest was strapped to the pony's back, but before Captain Snow departed he took down the musket that hung with its powder horn near the warm bricks of the chimney. He watched Jeremy oil and cock the gun, place its muzzle on the window ledge and lift its great weight to his shoulder.

"Never shoot till your grandaunt bids you," warned the Captain. "Then shoot to kill."

He unhitched Seesaw and led him down the road around the landward marsh. Jeremy and Bimini watched him go and Jeremy waved and sea-signaled until his father was out of sight. Then the boy's eyes looked sad. So Bimini, to distract his master, barked excitedly at a waxberry bush and made believe there was something under it. Jeremy paid no heed. Shading his eyes from the setting sun, he gazed down the empty road.

"Gr-r-r-r," growled Bimini loudly. Out with you! Up with you! and he dug ferociously into the sand. Suddenly, without any warning, with a motion rapid as light, something moved under the waxberry bush, something small with sharp bright eyes, something that vanished into the sand. A cold chill coursed through

Bimini. He dropped to a springing crouch. His little nose trembled with its effort to smell. What was this terrible, moving thing, this animal that was *not* an animal, for every living being has a scent that a dog can distinguish clearly, but this one left no trace on the wind, no taint on the bush that concealed it.

Cautiously Bimini withdrew from the bush. Soon he was sliding down-dune on the back of Jeremy's sand sled. He raced for sticks. He wagged his tail. He barked as gaily as usual, but every now and then a cold tremor moved across his fur like an icy hand, whenever he thought of that animal that darted from cover quicker than a fox, that disappeared into holeless sand, and that left no scent to follow.

The sun sank. April dusk came softly over the Dune Country.

"'Tis Sober Light, now," said Jeremy. That was the name that Cape people gave to the gray hour after sunset. "'Tis time we two went home."

Boy and dog made a last inspection of the Indian signal fire ready to be lighted on the Dune Before the Sea. For days before the Captain's departure Jeremy had built and rebuilt this small pile of driftwood logs. With it he planned to signal the *Abigail* when his father sailed her past the Dune Country, in the early hours of morning. Satisfied that the crossed logs were placed as he had left them, he set off over the dunes toward the house, pulling his sand sled behind him.

After what Aunt Samantha called a "consolation

supper" of samp and milk, baked fish and sweetened flour cake, Jeremy sat in front of the fire and said his lessons. Bimini stretched on the hearth. When the day's lessons were mastered and Bible-reading was over, Jeremy stirred restlessly. "Where's Long John?" he questioned.

"Gone to the Island," answered his grandaunt, "to take Maria the new wool for her weaving, and the meat and flour and rum and treacle that your father squanders his money for."

"Is it true, Grandaunt — what the village says — that Mistress Hallett is a witch?"

"Fol-de-rol! Silly maids' talk! Maria is only a poor girl who loved a blackhearted sailor."

"They say in the village, Grandaunt, that Mistress Hallett bewitched my mother but that she was too godly for Lucifer's liking, so he gave her back to the angels."

"Your mother and Maria were girls together. Close they were as sisters."

"Is it true, Grandaunt, that no living man dare put foot on her island?"

"No stranger can put foot there, Jeremy, ringed round as 'tis with 'tarnity sand, bogholes and quickmire."

"The sailors at Higgins Tavern, Grandaunt, say that the pirate, Samuel Bellamy, is sailing upcoast in a treasure ship to wed with Mistress Hallett."

"Upcoast, Jeremy. Never here! Too many hands, like mine, boy, itch to wring his neck."

When the hour came for slumber Bimini accompanied Jeremy into the upstep bedroom. While Jeremy knelt to say his prayers, Bimini pulled at the bedcovers; also he tried to get under them. He licked Jeremy's face. He pushed his way down the feather pillaber to a place near the footboard where three times he turned around to trample down a feathered nest into which he curled up neatly.

To the rolling drums of faraway surf, Jeremy fell asleep. Bimini dozed briefly. He was wakened abruptly by a glowing light that came through the seaward window. The full moon was summoning him, a great, heavy, golden moon. He lifted his head to bay its brightness. Then he remembered the scentless creature that disappeared under a bush. Making as little noise as he could with the soft pads of his paws, he jumped off the bed, landed on the braided mat and poked his nose around the corner of the upstep bedroom. Aunt Samantha sat by the fire, the good book drooping in her hand. Her head nodded, her eyes were closed; she was catching what she called a catnap.

Bimini slipped through the greatroom and into the summer kitchen. The outer door was on the latch awaiting Long John's return. He pushed the door open, wriggled through it and ran out into the night. He crossed Aunt Samantha's posy bed, and ambled down the seashell path that led to the road round the marsh. Long John's hut loomed dark in the moonlight close to the road's edge. He nosed his way to the back of the hut, headed into an open lean-to, then sprang aside just in time to avoid being hit by the flying hooves of the Indian pony, Seesaw. The pony had broken his halter. He had jumped his stall and with white-edged eyes was prancing out of the shed. He did not hear Bimini yelp. He did not see the small white figure crouched by the open door. Something was riding astride of his back, in form man-fashioned but scentless, with bright eyes and flapping ears and a feather in its red cap.

Without a glance toward the crouching dog, Seesaw galloped away. For a moment Bimini was too startled to move. Then like a flash he was off in pursuit as Seesaw turned toward the open Dune Country and headed toward the sea.

*   *   *

That was the night when the moon, Lilith, coiled at the full in heaven. Under her gaze the ocean swung like a pendulum strung to the beat of her pulse. Phosphorus fired the tidal surf. Bright moonwake spattered the bluewater.

In the full of her strength she gazed at the earth that was candlelit to her honor, and there she discovered an amber mist in the center of which a small house stood in a clearing, a gambrel-roofed house on an island of pines, aloof, enclosed, unshuttered.

"Child of time," said Lilith the Timeless, "Man from the first has thus forsaken us. Have I not given you skills beyond measure? Why do you wait to destroy him?"

Drawn by the moongaze over the pines, Maria stood close to her window. The moon that was climbing the eastern sky shone on her calm, white brows.

"For ten long years I have waited," said she, "steadfast, without the heart's veering. So Cape women have learned to wait. We are not afeered of time."

The slant-eyed serpent moon, Lilith, turned her gaze away from the island. She searched the broad seas till at last she discovered a tall, fair ship with her topsails spread, with a prow that cut clean through the fleck of the waves, ploughing a northerly course.

In the poop of the *Whidah* Sam Bellamy stood with his friend Paul Williams beside him. The two seamen kept watch side by side; they had been through much together. Paul, born and bred a Peninsula man, at dawn would take over a new command, the prize sloop *Postillion*. He lifted his head and sniffed at the wind. "Smells like Cape weather," said he — "salt to the lips, cool at the rib, but a warm hand plucking the heart-strings. There's a spicy tang to it sweeter far than the dizzified, flowery, spangled scents that bedew the tropic night.

"I have not been home these many years," he mused, and added ruefully, "'tis said my mother lies underground, my father's wits move slowly."

"Home!" echoed Sam Bellamy bleakly. To his mind's eye came the high steep cliffs of the east coast of Devon with a village crouched close to gray Channelwater and hedgerows budding in the April night and the primroses, bemused and foolish, opening to the moon's rays.

"Home!" The sound of it plucked at memory. To his mind's eye came a slender girl with blue-green eyes and corn-yellow hair and gentle hands and a glinting wit tempered like Spanish steel.

"She was a child when I wooed her," he thought. "Now she is woman of five and twenty, and many men have desired her. Yet never a message, writ or unwrit, have the sea couriers brought to me southward. Only the evil gossip — and the cruel tale of her stoning."

"Look aloft!" Into his sea partner's voice crept an urgent note of warning. Sam looked to the masts and spars. On the tips of the topmost yardarm two tiny flames, transparent at core, curled upward into the night.

"Saint Elmo's fire!" he exclaimed in wonder. "'Tis the first time I have ever beheld it though much 'tis spoke of at sea. The storm that blows northward, nipping our heels, is like to overtake us."

"Cape men call yonder the Sea Dobby Lights — portent of evil fortune."

"Speak soft!" cautioned the shipmaster. "There be trouble enow, afore the mast, with the discontents and mutterings roused by this northward voyage."

A sound of scurrying feet below turned their eyes to the hatch and the ladder. A grizzled head appeared at the hatch, followed by a slender figure in a landsman's kneebuckle suit. There were bright buckles, too, on his square-toed shoes and he held in his hand a peaked beaver hat like the burghers of Boston City.

With head thrown back he stared at the yardarms. The strong, fine lines of his face were gaunt in the moon's clear, frosty light.

"She has waited long. Now the hour draws nigh." He spoke in a low reflective voice, yet it carried on the still night air.

Paul Williams turned to his sea partner. "Daft he be, Sam. Ye should chain him below, lest he do ye some harm to the ship."

"'Tis ten long years," Sam answered his friend, "since I sailed through the bars of the Cape Country. None save this chartmaker knows how they drift — the terrible, wintry, changing drift that gives name to the outer bars of the Cape: *The Graveyard of the Sea.*"

"Why pin ye such faith on his charts, Sam?"

"I have tested him well. Daft he may be, but he handles the leads with a master hand, reads the sea flooring clear as a book, marks him the channels and shoals on his charts as exact as an etcher's line."

Barnabas Hobb, the chartmaker, gazed on at the glittering sea. Paul Williams who held him in curious hate lifted his voice to a sounding pitch, to goad the chartmaker's pride:

"We be nigher Cape waters than charts foretell!" — the chartmaker did not stir — "The *Whidah* has never touched northern port, yet yonder ride Sea Dobby Lights!"

"In the Old Country," said Bellamy, "such name we give to an impish folk who ride horses at night, steal vittles from larders and sleep in the lofts of stables."

"Yea, such they were once, — in the Old Country," answered his Cape-canny friend. "But the Great Sea Hook is Freedom's land. Two that came over with a horse from Whitby have set themselves up in the Dune Country. Had them a parcel of offspring, 'tis said, web-footed and huge of ear. These ride the night hawks and the ships at sea and coast up and down dune on duck-webbed feet when the moon is full-rigged and sailing."

"Such Old Wives' tales," jeered the black-browed pirate, "only Cape seadogs swallow. 'Tis the poured-down rum that has loosened their throats till they would not choke at a camel." He paused and stared at the yardarms. "Aloft rides Elmo's fire, I tell ye, a dropt-down mite from the roll of tempests. 'Tis sign of oncoming storm."

Paul Williams shook his head. Saint Elmo's fire he had seen in his youth, though he did not tell his captain this, for Sam was uneasy, quick-tempered, distraught, and his friend desired to calm him.

Barnabas Hobb turned with a start as if newly per-
ceiving the captains. He pointed his thin-fingered hand
to the spars, and spoke with a prophet's tone:

"Behold! Behold Saint Elmo's fire!"

"I told ye," said Sam to his sea partner.

The old man continued to speak undisturbed. "Oft
I have seen it in hours of storm but never before leaping up like a flame under the eyes of the moon."

Then the watch in the Crow's Nest cried a sail, a sail
off the port bows. The chartmaker hastened downladder again. The two on the poop deck grew taut
and still. The *Whidah* hove to. She reeled as she
swung. Her lights were doused; dark battens were
lifted; gun muzzles gleamed in the moonlight along
her slim, clean sides. Lithe-bodied sailormen swarmed
up the ratlines to reef the white topsails in. Then they
stared, stopped, hung poised in the rigging. Aloft two
pale betraying flames danced on the yardarm tips.

Sam Bellamy's quarterdeck voice rang out like a clap
of arrogant thunder. The men in the rigging stirred,
paused, then upward they jerked like puppets on a
string and the lights faded out on the spar tips.

"Dobbies be troublesome imps at most," Paul Williams reassured himself as he peered over the flickery
sea toward the new-cried, faraway sail. But his heart
kept drumming up in his throat:

Dobbies be witch familiars!

*   *   *

When Bimini reached the Dune Before the Sea he crouched in the shadow of the driftwood pile and gazed down a steep sand slope into Dune Valley below. Beyond this valley dropped a sheer sand cliff and a narrow ledge of black peat projected outward from the cliffside. Below the ledge the Great Beach curved like a silver ribbon of kelp, its far edge scalloped by waves, its near edge merging into Dune Country. Clumps of waxberry bushes dotted the stubble of sand in the Valley. Out of the tops of their glossy-leaved clusters, thin wisps of smoke spiraled upward into the moonblue night. Beside one of these bushes Long John's runaway pony stood surrounded by at least a dozen small figures with red caps, large ears and button-up North Country reefers.

Bimini edged further forward to the very rim of the marram grass that tufted the top of the high dune that overlooked Dune Valley. Though he wriggled ahead cautiously, to his dismay the ground gave beneath him and he and the whole forward crest of the dune moved rapidly into a sandslide. Faster and faster it carried him downward, no matter how he struggled, carried him to the foot of Dune Valley where he came up sharply against a waxberry bush.

Sand smarted his eyes, tickled his ears, gritted between his teeth. It stuck in his paws and dribbled through his tail, for he had rolled over and over again in an effort to right himself and to escape detection. A sand-wary dog, Peninsula born, would have known that the only thing to do, when one is caught in a long dune drift, is to float along with it peaceably, if possible right side up.

For a few moments he lay very still concealed by the soft white drift, while some half-dozen young goblins mounted the pony and rode him at gallop up to the edge of the cliff. Then they clung to his mane as he leaped in the air to land on the peat ledge below.

Down this sheer cliff to the ledge of dark peat Bimini had once watched Jeremy crawl, but he could not follow his master there for the straightaway drop was a hand-over-hand made by long sea-weathered spikes of wood driven deep in the cliff wall.

When the pony reached the seaward sand stretched taut as a sail by the unfurled tide, he bucked and stiffened, arched his neck and let fly with shining heels. Then a goblin from those who clung to his back let himself down by the halter rope, down among the flying hooves of the young moon-baited pony. The goblin held a cup in his hand, that looked to be carved out of wood.

Then Bimini, in a whipped-up state, forgot his plan to remain unseen and gave voice to a warning howl. He was startled by a clear, small voice that sounded close to his ear.

"Hush, little dog," said the bell-like voice. "This we have done for a thousand years. This we did before Caesar's legions marched over English soil."

Bimini whirled to face the sound and beheld a small

figure seated beside him and partly concealed by a waxberry clump which served as a sort of green thatched
roof for a dugout dwelling beneath it. Fear shot
through the dog. How could he keep any whereabout
track of such blowaway scentless creatures?

As the goblin spoke, bright liquid from the chalice
splashed on Seesaw's forehoof. A second flash and the
other forehoof was drenched in silver brew. The pony
reared, pawing the air. The halter rope swung down
his belly. The tiny goblin still clung to the end of it
and again from the chalice bright liquid fell on the
pony's two hind hooves.

Seesaw shivered, paused, quietened. The madness
was drawn out of him. And as Bimini watched in grave
alarm, up from the sand crept a waxy mist, over the
little pony's forelegs, over his quivering hind legs, over
his glossy hide. Soon he was coated with bluish waxberry almost as translucent as dawn. Day people could
not discern of him more than a blue shadow.

Bimini felt his fur stiffen. "Now I know who they
be," he thought, "Dobbies — Dobbies of Yorkshire!
'Tis a fine Yorkshire trick they have played. Seesaw's
done out of his rights!"

"It was *his* will," said the Dobby, reading the small
dog's thoughts. "If day people, of their own free choice,
forsake their kind, yet return at dawn to tell strange
tales to their fellows, then to save them from impris-
onment for madness we use a waxberry potion which
renders them invisible. Like the hair wreaths and the

waxed flowers they are preserved from withering and the brittle crumbling of age."

As he spoke the moon was darkened and a great bird flew across it. The night hawk circled Dune Valley, then slowly drifted downward, settling on a sand tuft not far from the Dobby's side. Off its back sprang a slender young goblin who ran across-sand and stood before the Ancient, his duck-feather cap in his hand.

"What news, young Hob?" asked the Elder.

"Strange tidings, Ancient. Captain Bellamy with a pirate escort, a fleet of seven captive vessels, is sailing the 'Paradise Bird,' the *Whidah,* northward on a course set to reach the Dune Country in a day."

"Who of us rides in the rigging?"

"Lobbin and Jack o' the Moon."

"What do they say of the Captain's plans?"

"On the open deck they heard him vow he would plunder the Cape, burn every house in Eastham village, punish the townsmen by death or as forced men for stoning Mistress Hallett as a witch. He swears he will wed her with ring and book on the teakwood decks of the *Whidah* and sail away to the Spanish Indies, she to be made Princess, there, of a West Indian Isle."

"What news to the north from the Province Lands?"

"The *Abigail,* Captain Snow in command, sets forth on the midnight tide."

"What is her course?" asked the Ancient.

"If the winds do not shift, by a thrice-turned glass she'll be in the midst of the pirates."

"Has the Captain been warned to change his course?"

"By spar lights we tried. By three black crows who alighted and screamed on the bowsprit. We soured the milk. We spread sand on the decks. But the Captain laughed at the croak of the crows. He ordered a sailor ashore for fresh milk. He washed the sand down the scuppers."

"Then there is no way," asked the Ancient, "by which we may warn him of danger?"

Bimini sprang to his feet. "The signal fire," he thought excitedly. "The signal fire on the dunes! Jeremy can warn him. I will waken Jeremy now!"

Again he was startled by a bell-like voice. "Go, little dog," said the Ancient with a crooked smile on his lips. "Go to the house Saint Godric guards. Warn Jeremy — if you can."

The moon rode high. The dunes shone white as Bimini whisked over them. The little house where Jeremy slept loomed dark against the horizon. At first Bimini ran with a gallant speed, then slowed his pace, then, before he came to the seashell path, paused and sat down to think. How was he to warn Jeremy? Carefully he went over all the things that a dog can do: bark; growl; whimper; bay; tug at Jeremy; lick his hand; dash to the door; carry a stick. Of what use were any of these accomplishments to tell a boy that he must signal news of pirates to his father? Of what use to a boy was his faithful dog if it could not warn him of evil?

After a long while Bimini crawled around to the back of the house. His tail was down between his legs. Even his head hung low. Near the door stood Jeremy's sand sled. Bimini curled up close beside it and put his nose on the pull-rope which Jeremy's hands had held.

Up in the sky the Twin Stars whispered. "Look," sighed Castor to Pollux, "look at the changing earth! On the yardarm tips where once our lights blazed in the Golden Age of Time now ride yon witch familiars!"

"Look," sighed Pollux to Castor, "look at the miserable earth! What sin did the dog commit in Eden to suffer so strange a fate?"

"He loved too well," said Castor. "He rendered up his soul."

"Bah," said the shining Dog Star Sirius, "pity him not! By that deed he is completed, unlike his master, man."

No voice from the sky came down to the little grieving dog in the dunes, but a soft breeze blew up from the marsh and Bimini whiffed the tang of it. Slowly he rose to his feet. He savored the eerie, salty smell of the swamp where animals spoke like men and courage returned to his furry body and to his loyal heart. Between his teeth he took the rope of Jeremy's sand sled. He tugged and pulled till it came about, pointing its prow toward the island. He dug in Aunt Samantha's posy bed and extracted his largest bone. This he placed on the seat of the sled. By these small signals he hoped that Jeremy would know where he had gone.

2

The Marsh Dwellers

THERE WERE three books in the jeweled chest over which Maria burned tallow: the Book of Uranus, the Heavens; the Book of Pluto, the Lodestone; the Book of Neptune, the Tides. From the Book of Uranus she learned to weave the web of the shifting winds. From the Book of Neptune she drew the knack of turning the ordered tides, and from it she brewed the potion that she poured one night in the marsh.

But the Book of Pluto, the Lodestone, haunted her sleep with dreams for, though she was wont to decipher its text, she dared not embark on the terrible secret its fine-lettered pages held. Yet hour by hour her keen brain reckoned the intricate computations.

Wisdom at best is a lonely art. Few give heed to it, many fear the venturesome minds that essay it. "Old Comer," said Maria grimly, "escape from God and from Lucifer gets man no nearer to freedom. 'Tis but a harsher lot we bear than any the Lord enjoins. To Him at least we might shift a load and now and again be clear of it."

"Ye have set yourself up as a god, Maria," answered the Little Old Man.

To the humble saltdwellers under the marsh, to the furred and winged folk of the island, Maria gave man's richest gift, the gift of human speech. And speech, she observed, like a candle mold, shaped the wax of their minds to its pattern, yet lay like tallow, a useless toy, till the wick of the will was tindered. Speech made the Marsh Dwellers closer of kin. They gathered together to hear themselves talk. They maneuvered for place, one with other. Thus in the marsh a kingdom formed, and grew set as a kingdom will, with a crotchety lobster for a gatekeeper and an old sea turtle for a king. Those who were born and bred to the swamp became hostile to all outside it, and the green-gold reeds and the tranquil pools were no longer a haven for wayfaring wings or a refuge for tidewater comers.

To Maria the Marsh Dwellers turned for aid and she learned to watch over her creatures, learned to accept their curious code built of trumpeting words and arrogant faith in the right of the dominant creed. But the deeper wisdom of forest and swamp they did not forsake completely, and Maria pondered the springs of their joy and their unconcern with dying.

"Hearken!" said she to the Old Comer. "Speech that is ever the mark of man brings a finer life to the marsh."

"I hear," answered the Old Comer, "only the Marsh Dwellers still, only the flotsam of time, Maria, who have no souls to trade."

*　　*　　*

When Bimini entered the treachery swamp he prudently picked up Long John's scent, for the Indian, within a tide's reach, had been traveling the hidden path. The trail led from his hut to swampwater, circled its edge for a short distance, then doubled back over a sandhill and dropped into a thicket of pines. At the foot of these pines, hidden from view, a small finger of the marsh curved inland. Through the center of this dark inlet stretched a narrow bar of sand.

Following the moccasin trail closely, Bimini ventured out on the bar. The footing was firm. On either side black mudholes yawned and stagnant pools were thick with a green scum. He sniffed his way along the bar, being careful to tread as nearly as he could in the prints of Long John's moccasins. On either side of the hidden path the marshwater grew deeper. The mud at the shoreline disappeared and the protection of the pine grove gave way to a screen of tufted reeds as high as a man's head.

He followed the scent steadily for some half-turning of an hourglass, then stuck his nose between the reeds to look out at a pool of deep water. Clear green, lighted within, it shone like a candlelit window. In its depths he perceived a large lobster swaying back and forth on the marshbottom with a curious, mincing gait. Beside the lobster gleamed a pair of rusty, lensless spectacles and in front of him a narrow logbook lay open on the sand flooring, its pages covered with entries in a small, cramped hand. Then up from the seabottom came a voice, speaking the language of man. "Dog *one*; Dog, *white*," it said, and the lobster bent over the log.

Bimini had but a poor opinion of the natural wits of tide scrabble. He hurried forward, head down, intent, absorbed in his tracking. After a while he was brought up abruptly by the total disappearance of the scent under a ripple of water. Where the path ended the reeds opened out forming a large circle, in the center of which, like a gleaming jewel, lay a moon bright pond.

There was nothing for it but to swim across. Bimini plunged into cold green water and swam toward the opposite shore. He was halfway across when he noticed an eddy of moon ripples moving on the pool's surface, and a flat head with ears laid back swam at the prow of the ripples. Bimini took one anxious look. This, he decided, was a water rat, and he swam toward shore the harder. For with all the grave issues that weighed on his wits, he dared not mix in a fight.

Then something caught hold of his paw, piercing deep into the flesh of it, pulling him under the surface. Bimini tried to tear its grip loose, but he could not crack the hard shell and a huge claw dug into him. He continued to swim with this menace attached, but its weight kept pulling his head under water. He observed that the rat was coming toward him, hopeful-eyed, swimming steadily. To a terrier dog a rat is an almost irresistible temptation. Every instinct in Bimini yearned to do battle with the rat.

Then the shore came up suddenly under his feet, a smooth level strand of it. He stood up, shook himself. With the pool water still cold on his legs he reached down, bit hard, and with a tremendous toss of his head, he yanked off a big sea crab. The momentum of this effort flung the crab in front of him on shore. To his horror, directly beneath it, the sand opened up and the crab disappeared as if dropped in a pot on the fire.

Tensely, alert to all manner of scents, Bimini sniffed at the quicksand, trying to get the tang of it as a warning against its evil. But the terrible bog sand had no separate scent discernible from the poolwater.

He stood very still and gazed at the shore. His paw was bleeding where the flesh was pulled out of it, and the cold salt water of the pool stung the wound like a wasp. There was nothing for it but to turn about and swim away from the shore.

He paddled cautiously around the sedges, trying to pick up Long John's scent, peering ahead at the glinting water, cocking his eye at the rat. It was drifting lazily toward the center of the pool, watching him with a beady eye. Dimly the thought occurred to Bimini that the rat would know where the quicksands were and might by attack be forced in flight to reveal a place of safe landing.

Swimming with eager, renewed purpose he circled around the rat. It remained, on guard and watchful, and kept turning slowly, grimly, to face the movements of the dog. When Bimini felt that the shoreward path was a safe retreat at his back, he started forward, his neck-hair bristling, his ears flattened for the fray. As he swam he growled with increasing volume, like the rumble of approaching thunder. The rat stayed in the center of the pond and showed two yellow fangs.

"I am Death coming," rumbled Bimini fiercely. "By the Laws of our Kind 'tis death to the rat to fight a Scots dog."

"By the Laws of the Marsh," said a thin voice coolly, "our kind die only by the Witch's will. 'Tis you, little dog, who face death."

"Then I'll die in the fight as my fathers before me!" growled Bimini and lunged for the rat.

The water roiled. There was nothing at all in the grip of his clenched jaws. "I cannot have missed him," thought Bimini wildly. "I have never before missed a kill!" And he rose to the surface and looked quickly round for signs of the yellow-fanged rat. Nothing was there save moon bright water and the hissing whisper of the reeds.

Suddenly, far to the right of the shoreward path, something gray-brown slunk into the grasses. Bimini swam toward it swiftly, but with a Scot's true caution he slowed his paddling and lifted his nose to sniff and sniff at the shore. Faint yet clear the man-scent came to him, token of Long John's trail.

Once more following moccasin prints, Bimini nosed along, keeping his eye on flanking reeds lest the rat attempt an ambush. After a long interval of progress he was stopped by a harsh command:

"Halt, young dog. None passes here save at the will of Snake-eye."

A tremendous chorus of all kinds of voices took up the echoing challenge: "The will of Snake-eye! — Snake-eye!"

Bimini lifted his head. A high rock jutted over the path. Back of it loomed the dark pines of an island. In front the path opened out to a beach yellow with reflected moonlight. Ranged on either side of the rock, in a semicircle that extended swampward till it reached the edge of the thinning reeds, a large assembly of animals had gathered.

Nearest the rock from which the voice issued, all sizes of turtles perched, seated in rows on a rough

pile of rotting driftwood logs. On the other side of
the rock a dozen water rats sat on their haunches,
wrangling among themselves. One or two babies, out
of hand, kept skittering across the circle. Next to the
water rats crouched a group of fluffy black and white
colony animals which Bimini knew to be skunks. A
large family of woodchucks in back of them peered
over their heads, and a huge raccoon, whose eyes in the
moonlight looked as big as Aunt Samantha's cookies,
had stretched himself along the limb of the pine tree
nearest to the beach.

On the other side of the semicircle, next to the
turtles, came crabs, hordes of crabs, big ones, little
ones, arriving late in scuttling batches and moving
together, now this way, now that, as if in a series of
misdirected military formations. Next to the crabs,
snakes had foregathered, both water and land snakes, a
few lying extended in the moonlight but the majority
coiled, their dark heads weaving back and forth in a
dizzying rhythmic pattern. From the height of some of
their heads Bimini realized that the black snakes were
of a considerable size, but none of them compared
remotely with the tremendous, swaying python directly
below the rock.

Suddenly the rock itself, or at least a large part of
the top of it, moved slowly forward and a huge head
with baleful eyes thrust itself over the ledge. This was
an old sea turtle, with a high-backed furrowed shell,
so salt-rimmed, scarred and hoary that it seemed a part

of the rocky throne from which he ruled his realm.

With the trail ahead unknown, unseen, with treachery sand behind him, Bimini knew that only his wits stood betwixt him and disaster. Casting about for a trick or device he remembered how he himself had been awed by the sight of Seesaw's white-rimmed eyes when the pony broke loose from the shed.

Wrenching his gaze from the frightening groups of animals that faced and flanked him, he stared up into the full of the moon and wailed at the top of his howl:

"Woe to the beast that molests me! Moon maddened I am and fey!"

He looked down quickly and cocked an eye to gauge the effect of this effort.

"What does he say? What does he say? What is the little dog yowling about?" demanded the huge sea turtle in the echoing language of man. "The Witch does us an evil turn," he grumbled, "depriving us of our native tongues."

The black snake, coiled beneath the rock, swaying its head back and forth like an anchor rope, spoke in soft sibilant tones.

"My lord, my lord, have a care!" said the snake. "What need have we Islanders for the speech of common creatures?"

"Tamar, fawning Tamar!" sneered Snake-eye. "Bring me Fang Ho, the Rat."

"Here, my lord, here," said a squeaky voice and

the rat that Bimini had fought in the pool stepped into the center of the circle.

"Can ye still speak the animal tongue, Fang Ho?"

"Aye, my lord," answered the rat, "I have already reviled with sharp words the ancestors of the dog."

"Unfair! Unfair!" hooted an owl in a pine tree back of the rock. "Why should the rat speak animal language and we have only this silly man-speech which holds no wisdom of the forest in it and none of the passwords of the night?"

"Be still!" thundered Snake-eye.

" 'Twas a fair bargain," whined Tamar. "So long as the rat stays away from the cheese, the Witch grants him animal tongues. But it will not be for long, for long." He began to weave his head back and forth, staring fixedly at the rat. "There's a new cheese in the Witch's hut, a beautiful — soft — golden — cheese. Long John brought it, this day."

The rat stared fascinated at the snake, which slowly without unwinding its coils, approached him with lowering head.

"Hoot," mocked the owl in the tree. "Hoot, Tamar! Take your evil eye off Fang Ho, or I'll fasten my talons in your writhing back and crack your spine like a faggot."

" 'Tis the right trick to kill him!" thought Bimini. "The owl is a knowful bird."

"Fang Ho," said Snake-eye, "bespeak the young dog.

Tell him into whose kingdom he comes. Ask him what forfeit he will pay for his life?"

The rat turned to Bimini. "What say you, Biteless Terrier?" he jeered. "Make answer to Snake-eye's question."

Bimini spoke very slowly. "I desire to learn the speech of man before the hour of Sun-coming. As for ransom — I am new come to this land. I have naught save three buried bones."

"What does he say, Fang Ho?"

"He says he will eat us and bury our bones," answered Fang Ho politely.

"Rat," said Bimini, "you shall pay for this."

"Hoot, hoot!" screeched the owl in the tree. "Fang Ho, he lies. No dog ever flung such defiance without his neck-hair bristling."

He flew down to a limb of the tree that protruded over the sand. "Will you fight for your life, little dog?" said he. "If so, lift your right paw."

Bimini lifted his paw. Blood from the crab bite dropped on the sand — three dark blots of it.

"S-so, he iss wounded," hissed Tamar the Snake.

"It was I who conquered him in battle," boasted Fang Ho. "I fought him in the Green Pool."

"Ye lie! Ye lie! Fang Ho, he lies." A hundred little voices took up shrieking denial. "We crabs, we did it. We were there! We know!"

"Wounded or not," said Snake-eye, "the dog has

agreed to fair fight. If he wins he passes; if he loses
he dies. 'Tis the Law of our Kind."

"Leave the dog to me," whined Tamar. "I will hug
the breath out of his puffy white body. I will strangle
that dismal howl."

"And what of Fang Ho?" said Snake-eye with a
gleam in his lidded glance. "He, who has defeated
him once, has a first right to the battle."

"My lord," said Fang Ho in a virtuous tone, "I
have had my sport. Let some other of the Islanders
know the triumph of beating a dog."

"I would fight him myself," said Snake-eye, "but I
be too old to strike."

"Am I not born to succeed you?" whined Tamar.
"Let me succeed you in the fight."

Bimini's heart stood still. He had no idea how
large Tamar was, but from the height of the swaying
head poised over the pulsing coils, Bimini knew he
would have to leap high, at incredible speed, with un-
flinching force, to fasten his teeth into Tamar. And
if he should leap and yet fail of his grip, he knew that
the snake's great lapping coils would entwine him and
choke off his breath.

"Let Tamar fight!" shrieked the water rats.

"Aye, aye," called out turtles and crabs.

"Good enough, good enough," grumbled the woodchucks.

"Tamar it shall be!" said Snake-eye.

"Tamar! Tamar!" yelled the swamp people. "Yeh, Tamar! Have at him!"

Everything was against Bimini. Sand burned like fire in his wounded paw. His body felt wet and heavy. Worst of all he was placed at the bottom of a sand slope, which dropped so sharply that no spring of his young muscles would permit him to make a fast kill.

Wasting no strength on threats or boasts, he limped forward and stood at slight crouch, his hind legs moving delicately as he tested the strength of his ground. Tamar uncoiled in the moonlight. He seemed to Bimini as long as a ship, a horrible, thickening, undulant power that poured itself over the sand.

"Look at me, dog! Look at me," he crooned in a low, singsong whine. He began to coil and uncoil, to twist and sway, and ever his head with its double-lidded eyes and its darting tongue wove back and forth in front of the dog's nose. For a moment Bimini felt creep over him the moveless spell of snake sorcery. His gaze grew vague and bland. Then a screeching voice from a pine bough broke in with a loud complaint. "Unfair! Unfair!" shrieked the yellow-eyed owl. "Cease spellbinding the dog, Tamar! You challenged him to *fight*."

A black snake, like a python, kills by hugging the enemy, but first he tries to entice his victim into a maundery trance. Then he strikes a driving blow with the head, and in the moment of reeling shock, he gathers his victim into the coils of his powerful, writhing body.

Thanks to the owl, Bimini was wakened from the dangers of enticement. He began to circle the snake, warily, trying to get to the upper beach, essential for a leaping kill. Tamar recognized his tactics and blocked him at every turn.

"I must get him off guard, somehow," thought Bimini. "If only the owl would hoot again!"

Suddenly the snake darted a javelin-like blow with its head. The dog leaped aside in time. The hard head slid past his wet smooth coat. Seizing the chance Bimini hurled himself forward and gained the upper beach. The sand slope was now in his favor.

"Let him thrust his head at me once again! I'll crack his spine in two!" Bimini was warming to the pace of the fight and it brought increase of courage.

To Tamar the downward slope was no disadvantage. If anything, it gave him a better level from which to dart his blows.

"Die, s-silly dog," he hissed, and feinted a quick, forward thrust, hoping to draw Bimini into an ill-timed sidewise leap. But the dog stood fast and waited tensely, his haunches gathered under him, his eyes following every motion of the snake's weaving head.

"Have at him, Tamar!" squeaked Fang Ho. "This be no dance of the herons!"

"At him, Tamar! At him!" shrieked the Marsh

Dwellers, and Bimini realized that the snake was listening, suddenly aware of the watchers. Then Tamar
began to sway again, with deadly purpose, with light-
ning speed, and with an increase of showmanship.

"He is vain," thought Bimini. "He will drive at me
soon. The Marsh Dwellers are growing impatient. He
is making display to his people."

The swaying became more intense.

"S-so s-strikes Death," hissed Tamar, and his head
shot forward like a driven spear.

Bimini sprang. His sharp teeth dug into the snake's
skin directly behind the head, and with the full force
of his leap to aid him, he bit into Tamar's back. For
a moment dog and snake swirled madly in a storm of
sand and fury. Bimini held fast to his prey. His body
was hurled off the ground, flung this way and that,
bruised, thrashed, but never quite encircled. Then he
felt the spine of the great snake snap, and an intoler-
able twitching weight hung fastened, clenched in his
jaws. All the anger repressed in his hour of danger now
swept in bleak fury upon him. He snarled, growled,
tried to lift and worry and destroy the jerking body,
but the great snake was too heavy for him. Dimly
through the heat of combat he began to be aware of
tumult and shouts that echoed round him.

With effort, slowly, for his jaw muscles had stiffened,
Bimini loosened his grip.

"Well done, Dog," said Snake-eye, a new respect in
his voice. "Perchance ye are destined to succeed

Tamar. Come, sit with me here on the rock awhile
and gaze upon my people."

Bimini looked at Snake-eye's jaws. They were
clamped like a hunter's trap. He turned to the rat.
"Tell Snake-eye," said he, "that a dog's paws slip on a
rock's smooth surface. Tell him I cannot climb."

He observed that Fang Ho this time translated his
words correctly. "And now," he said, "explain to your
King that I must go to the Witch."

"To the Witch!" cried the Marsh Dwellers. "To
the Witch he would go!" And they shook their heads
in wonder.

"To the Witch he shall go," said Snake-eye. "The
owl, his friend, shall lead him."

The semicircle of animals opened at the center and
Bimini saw a narrow path leading into the Island.

"This way, this way," hooted the owl.

Bimini limped badly, but he kept his head up, his
ears pricked, and his tail erect, held gallantly, as befits
a Scots Highlander. Nevertheless he was more than
thankful when at last the dark path hid him from the
countless, sharp, staring eyes of the assembled Marsh
Dwellers.

3

The Witch

WHEN Bimini and the owl reached the house of Mistress Hallett, the owl perched on the peak of its gambrel roof while Bimini mounted the doorstone and scratched with his paw on the door.

"Who waits without?" called a soft voice.

He scratched again, politely, making the sound small and friendly, for he was all too aware that within these walls lived not only a sorceress but a wolf.

The door opened, revealing a woman with a lighted candle in her hand. Her eyes were like the deeps of Gull Pond. Her hair was like corn silk at Sun-coming. Yet over Bimini crept an eerie warning of her strangeness, though she was the most beautiful woman that he had ever seen. And Maria Hallett of Eastham Parish had never seen a dog like Bimini, for terriers were rare in the young colony and he was the first Scots Highlander ever to come to America.

"Good evening, little dog," said Maria. "What brings you here, tonight?"

Bimini gazed at her solemnly, then he lifted his voice in a howl.

"Marcy upon us!" Maria said. " 'Tis a strange time-o-night to come calling on folk who live in a miry bog!"

Then she observed the blood on his coat and the drops that fell from his paw.

"Come in, little dog," she said gently. "I do not know what your eyes are asking. I cannot speak your tongue."

Despair swept over Bimini. Surely a witch who could bespell a marsh ought to possess sufficient sorcery to understand a dog.

He limped over the doorsill. A great gray beast lying by the hearthside rose slowly to its feet. Two pale yellow eyes stared vacantly at the dog, and again Bimini felt creep over him the eerie sense of strangeness.

"Lie down, Wu Wang," said Maria Hallett. "The dog is wounded. He comes to our door. He has the right of sanctuary."

She opened a cupboard, took out a small roll of clean linen, a jar of ointment and a wash cloth. She dippered some water from a bucket into a small basin and summoned Bimini to her side.

He took hold of the rim of her skirt with his teeth. He pulled at it gently, firmly. Maria stared gravely down on him. She was puzzled by his look of unflagging purpose; she wondered at his tenacity; but nothing in her ancient spell books had given her the answer to his need.

She lifted the small dog on her lap to wash his bleeding paw. He made no protest, neither winced nor whimpered as she opened, cleansed and bound his wound. After the wound was bandaged, she laid her hand on his head. "Look ye," she said, "there's a faraway chance that what you wish to tell to me may be said in man's clumsy speech. Such skill I have power to give to you — but only at the price of memory."

Bimini paid no heed to her warning. All he heard was the wished-for words. His tail thumped; his body wriggled. He licked her cheek; he licked her hand; he quivered with hope and expectancy.

She stroked his soft white head.

"I have wanted a dog," said Maria Hallett, "ever sence I was young."

She roused herself and spoke to Bimini in a clear, quiet voice. "Hearken closely, little dog," said she. *"The speech of man that I give to you comes at the price of memory.* If you speak like man you will be, like man, deef to all other animals. Like man, you will find yourself false to your past, caring too much for your future. Chained forever to the marsh and this island, you will do my bidding and serve me only, so long as the spell endures."

For the first time in his brave young life Bimini cowered with fear. What was the use of the tongue of man if he were to forget his master?

Then he recalled that he, the dog, was different from all other creatures. He belonged to Jeremy completely. No power in heaven, no fiend in hell could alter that simple fact.

Maria stroked his quivering body with hands long empty of love, till she felt the fear die away in his breast and sensed his consent to the bargain.

She set Bimini down on the hearth. The wolf stirred restlessly. From a jeweled chest she took a thick book and a small, delicate vial. These she placed on a table under the drip-torch glow. She sighed as she worked. "Dog," said she, "by ill-hap I have learned 'tis the saddest of all earth's practices for which you sell your soul. Made with the unruly lips and tongue, it all too often fails to convey the message of heart and brain."

"I wish she would hasten," thought Bimini, keeping his eye on the wolf. "I am not well placed on this narrow hearth if Wu Wang takes it into his head to play a part in this spell-making."

The Witch read aloud in very low tones a page from the old book. Then she rose and opening the vial dropped on Bimini's soft, furry head a single drop of a very cold liquid that numbed his brain and caused a sharp pain in his heart. Two drops from the vial she flung in the fire. It flared suddenly upward, and Bimini turned to look.

In a hearthfire the blaze is like yellowy air, bright and clear-seeming, yet it cannot be pierced by the eye. Whereas these flames were transparent, and in them people were moving about as if in a mirrored reflection.

In one flame four puppies sprawled folded over one another, lapped in luxuriant sleep. Vaguely Bimini remembered that these were his litter brothers. In another flame he saw a tall man with laughing blue eyes and a rueful smile, and a spy glass held in his hand. Beyond him, an old woman paced back and forth in front of a loom, her black eyes snapping, her bonnet strings tied crisply under her chin. The flames shot higher. Clear in their heart appeared a small boy with a white, drawn face, a boy standing on the edge of the marshwater, calling over the swamp.

"My master! My master!" yelped Bimini and was astonished to hear a young voice that echoed through the greatroom, crying, *my master! my master!*

Out of the fire the figures went, fading like ghosts at dawn. Only the flames burned on, still transparent but empty, and as Bimini searched them eagerly, something of their blank transparency crept into his warm brown eyes until their depths no longer held the soft look of devotion.

"Master! Master!" he cried in a voice that rang with new despair.

Maria knelt beside him. Tears swam like stars in her sea-blue eyes, but her words, as she spoke, were firm and steady, and her hand was gentle on his coat.

"Mistress is the word," she said, "Little Dog Who Speaks Like a Man."

"No! No!" cried Bimini. "Master!"

"And who is he?" asked the Sea Witch.

Bimini turned and looked at her with a vacant gaze like Wu Wang's, except that his contained within it a haunting, baffled protest. "I do not know," he answered slowly, "but him alone I serve."

"Lie down by the hearth," said the Witch, gently. "Rest, little dog, from your journey."

Bimini lay down on the hearth opposite Wu Wang. He felt neither fear nor interest now in the great gray wolf. He wondered why his body ached, and why his paw was wounded. When the Witch brought him a plate of corn mush, he lapped a little, though he suffered no hunger. He put his nose down on his sandy paws and dozed a while, and growled in his dream, and the feeling of exhaustion left him.

The Witch sat by the table, reading her ancient book. Now and again she glanced over at him as if she desired to speak. But what it might be that she thought of saying, the little dog who could speak like a man neither knew nor cared.

An owl hooted in the night. There was something familiar in the sound of it, some unexplained summons to action that brought the dog to his feet. He walked slowly, as if in a dream, to the door of the hut and scratched on it. Maria Hallett rose from her reading and quietly opened the door.

Bimini stepped across the doorstone. Over him wheeled the stars.

"Look," whispered Castor to Pollux, "at the door of our Sister's house!"

"Lackaday," answered Pollux to Castor, "the little dog's eyes are quenched!"

"But his heart," said the Dog Star, Sirius, "beats undismayed in his breast."

*   *   *

Bimini stood still for a time while he savored the scents of the island.

"Hoot, hoot," sang a yellow-eyed owl perched on the roof of the house.

"Owl," said Bimini, "knowful ye be, traveling about by night. Where sleeps the house where my master bides? Oh, who, *who* is he?"

"Who? Who? Who?" sang the owl.

"Bury my bones," growled Bimini, "this world is a mixed-up place!"

"Come — come — come," called the owl, and he flew from the rooftree down along a dark path, back to a pine tree near the door, and then again down the path. All the while he hooted mournfully as if lamenting fate.

Bimini followed slowly down the turns of a pine-dark trail. He sniffed at the moist needle-ground of the earth, at the feathery brush, at the windy air. The owl continued to fly before him, inviting him to follow.

After a while, the path opened out into a moon-yellowed beach. Beyond this glimmered a marsh. A large stone jutted over the path, and halfway down the scuffed up sands the body of a great black snake lay caught in twisted death. "This," thought Bimini, "I have seen before." And he stood very still and tried to recall the living look of the snake.

"Hush, hush," whispered the reeds.

"Remember, remember," rippled the water.

"Lost, lost," sighed the wind.

A cracked voice shattered his revery.

"Well, dog," said the voice fretfully, "what brings you doubling back on your tracks? Are you afraid of the Witch?"

"I am trying to find," said Bimini, "the scent of my lost master, and the path that leads toward home."

The harsh voice from the top of the rock burst into a jeering chuckle.

"Dog," said the voice, "you serve a witch. You have no master now."

Bimini looked up and perceived a giant turtle on the rock's high ledge.

"Turtle," he answered, "I am a dog, different from

all other animals." And he continued onward, down the beach, toward a point where the tall reeds parted.

Again the turtle cackled. Then Bimini felt creeping over him a stiff, unaccountable backward pull as if he were chained as once he had been on board a swaying ship. Forcing ahead against this drag, he gave the dead snake a wide berth, but as he reached the lower beach all power of forward motion left him and he stood, straining, straining, as dogs have stood for endless hours since they first belonged to man.

He remained motionless for a very long time, until light broke over the paling sky. Slowly the red sun rose. Far away on the seaward horizon a thin column of smoke mounted. At sight of it Bimini trembled with a sense of broken destiny.

"What a queer animal dog is," mused Snake-eye from his sentry rock as he watched the dog standing at point, blindly resisting enchantment. "They get their minds set on somebody else. They have no souls of their own."

Aloud he called in a voice more kindly than was his wont to use: "It is of no avail, dog, to break your body against unseen chains. Come back. Sit under the rock awhile and tell me a tale of the kingdom of men, the fitful, hungersome creatures ye serve, who rile our peaceable seas."

As if in a dream Bimini turned, climbed the sand beach, lay down below the rock. He glanced with puzzled eyes at the snake then turned his grave, lackluster gaze back to the column of smoke.

The Book
of
Jeremy

1

The Boy Seeks His Dog

W<small>HEN</small> the little dog left the house on the island the hour was close to Sun-coming. Maria did not return to her bed; she paced up and down the great-room, struck by a sharp misgiving.

"What have I done?" she chided herself as she thought on the haunted look of the dog. "Too readily I have come to use the powers that lead to darkness. Dog is the loving friend of man and I craved his love with envy. Lonely I be that thus I seek to sever his bonds to his master!

"The years drift by me like wind-driven fog," continued Maria sadly. "Abigail's boy is now nine and a

117

half. At ten he will follow his father to sea. Ten is
the due age for seafaring."

For the thousandth time she recalled to her mind
how she rocked the child in his cradle, how he curled
his small hand tight round her finger when she fed
him the warm milk posset. With a sudden look of
purpose she turned and went downstep to the jeweled
chest that stood by the head of her bed. There she
paused, opened the lid, and lifted out a tiny vial concealed in the chest's till.

"I will summon him now," she whispered. " 'Tis
time that he come to me now."

She recalled that Jeremy's eyes were blue, like
Abigail's eyes but a softer shade with a shining glow
that waked when he smiled to gay and dancing fire.
She thought of the little dog's warm, sweet gaze and of
how her spells had emptied his eyes when the sorcery
overtook him.

Slowly, as if her white hand had stiffened, she replaced the vial in the chest.

"Jeremy! Jeremy!" she exclaimed. "Better I never
should see your face!" and she knelt by the bedroom
window.

Over the sea the sun rose up. The air was gold and
green. A thin finger of smoke mounted from the faraway Dune Before the Sea. It billowed upward, a
slender shaft, then broke into puffs like a signal fire.
Maria watched it closely.

When the smoke signals had drifted away and

clearly the sun upshone, she put the kettle on the fire and climbed upladder to the loft. Soon she returned with her father's worn Bible and this she placed on the table.

"Lord," she prayed, as she knelt by the hearth to cook breakbroth and samp, "Lord, though black be the sins of men, Ye have never brought into human eyes the look of the sorceried creatures! If my magic I yield to Your Immanent Power, will Ye bring to me Abigail's boy?"

*   *   *

When morning came to the Dune Country Jeremy awoke. The sun was almost horizon high. Scudding clouds, moving north by east, flickered over the ocean like a school of gilded fish.

"Bimini," said Jeremy. Nothing moved on the pillaber.

"Bimini," Jeremy whispered clearly. The bed covers did not stir. Jeremy sat up in bed.

"Bimini!" he called for the third time. Nothing crawled out from under the bed where Bimini loved to hide.

As fast as he could, Jeremy dressed. Calling softly he ran through the house. He opened the back door and whistled. There came no answering patter of feet, no low affectionate growl. His gaze fell on the sand sled. He had not left it there on the hill, headed toward the island. Nor left that dirty, smelly bone lying on the seat of the sled.

Troubled, aware that time was passing when he should be making the hearthfire, putting on the kettle for Aunt Samantha, fetching water from the well; aware, too, that shortly after dawn the *Abigail*, tacking against a light head wind, would be sailing past the Dune Before the Sea, Jeremy ceased his search for Bimini and hastened through his chores. Then he thrust a piece of breakbread into his pocket, took a homespun blanket left waiting by the settle, and a box of tinder and flint. With these he ran rapidly over the dunes to the driftwood pile on the Dune Before the Sea. He struck fire as the sun came up. A small sloop on the landward tack was driving straight toward the Dune Country.

"The *Abigail!*" yelled Jeremy, and he jumped up and down and madly fanned the fire till he scorched a corner of the blanket.

Smoke rose crookedly, blowing north in the line of the soft cloud drift, a slender shaft not steady as it should be, but the boy could wait no longer. He began to pass the blanket over the column of smoke.

At the rail of the *Abigail* Captain Snow stood with the mate at his side. The Captain put a spy glass to his eye.

"I can see the boy clearly," he said, "but I can't make out the dog."

He passed the glass to the Mate. "Can ye pick up a bundle of white," said he, "about the size of a bunched skysail? It should be leaping about the boy's legs."

"I see the boy by the fire, sir. I can't descry any dog."

Smoke began to billow and puff. The blanket was passing over it.

"Here come the signals," said Captain Snow, and he put the sea glass up to his eye and faithfully counted the puffs.

"What does he say?" asked the Mate, smiling, when the smoke signals had ceased.

"He says, 'All's Well.' " said the captain of the *Abigail*. "God grant it remain so."

He unfurled a bright ship's pennant, let it stream along the sloop's rail. Jeremy waved the blanket. Then the little *Abigail* swung over, and turning her bows to the seaward tack, she headed into the sun.

Jeremy sat by the fire. He took a piece of break-bread from his pocket and tried to eat it but the bread was dry and seemed to stick in his throat. He banked the signal fire with sand, a task barely completed when from the house a ship's bell clanged. It occurred to Jeremy that Bimini might hear the loud summons of the ship's bell and hurry home for breakfast.

*   *   *

"What makes your eyes red?" snapped Aunt Samantha as Jeremy pulled off his sea jacket.

"Smoke," said Jeremy.

"Where's your dog?"

"He's gone. He's gone away."

"Nonsense," said Aunt Samantha. "He's much too fond of his vittles."

"Maybe the Indians stole him, Grandaunt."

"He's not that much of a dog."

"He left in the night. Do you think the wolf got him?"

"I think he's off chasing a moor rabbit. Before the day's out he'll come dragging home with thorns in his paws and burrs in his ear and a pick-thread look in his eye."

As soon as breakfast was finished, Jeremy stacked the dishes and went out to do the barn chores. As he passed the sand sled, he looked at it again. Why was the dirty bone there? Who moved his sled in the night? He stooped and examined the pull-rope closely. Sharp little teeth marks had dug at the center of it. So Bimini had moved his sled! For the second time Jeremy noted that it pointed toward the island.

After the barn chores were done, he went to Long John's house to ask the help of the Indian in his search for Bimini. Long John was not at home. Fresh paw marks led from the doorstone in the direction of the marsh. They followed Long John's moccasin prints, overstepping them clearly. Had Bimini trailed Long John to the marsh? Had the Indian become bogged in quicksand and Bimini heard him call. A surge of excitement swept through Jeremy. He searched the ground thoroughly. There were no returning footprints to be found of either dog or man. Long John and Bimini were both in the marsh and neither had returned from it!

Jeremy went to the swamp's edge and peered over

its shining reeds. The island looked dark and near.

"The tides have not come over their tracks. I could follow their footprints in safety," thought Jeremy. "I could find them — if I dare."

"Dare — Dare!" whispered the reeds. A big frog boomed, "Come along, come along!" A little fish leaped in the marshwater. The ripples sang, "Lost, lost."

As far as Jeremy could see in the swamp there was no sign of Bimini, no sign or sound of Long John.

"I must track them, find out how they entered the swamp," thought Jeremy, and stooping to examine their footmarks was surprised to find that instead of continuing toward the island on the slender, shining bar of sand that stretched outward from shore, the tracks of man and dog turned abruptly and headed toward a pine-covered hill.

On the other side of this hill the marsh protruded far into the land, a long, muddy finger of it. He lost the prints in brown needle-ground as he climbed over the hill slope, but he found them again on the downward side where the pines yielded to a narrow inlet of quagmire holes and bogwater.

His promise to his father to keep well away from the treachery swamp kept echoing in his ears. But with Bimini lost and Long John too, with one or both of them quickmired, what kind of boy was he to linger? If he found them, even a boy might save them, or summon help in time.

"Father," he said, speaking aloud as if the Captain

could hear him. "Father, the time has come for me to enter the Golden Marsh."

He waited a moment as often he did when he spoke aloud in this way. Sailor fathers are seldom at home, and they have to be consulted somehow. The feeling of an answer came.

He took off his cobblered shoes. These were costly in the New Colony, and Jeremy knew, if his shoes were mired, Aunt Samantha would be angry. Also she might not be able to expend the extra shilling and six-pence that Mr. Higgins, the cobbler, required for a new pair.

He knotted the deerhide lacings together, shoe to shoe, so that each was attached to its mate. He wadded his stockings firmly into the tips of their toes, then slung the shoes round his neck.

Like all the sons of Cape sailormen, Jeremy wore long trousers of wool, the legs widely bell-bottomed so that they rolled up readily for wading, or dusty road walking, or for doing of household chores. He rolled his trousers up to his thighs as high as they would go, then footed it down to the bottom of the slope where he stuck one toe into the chill mud-brown water of the bog. It felt like winter ice.

Carefully checking the trail he must follow, he entered the marsh along a narrow strip of sand. On this he had not traveled more than a quarter-turn of the hourglass when he was startled by a droning sound like voices raised in a chantey. At the sound his heart

ran about in his breast and he sought for a useful
weapon. A driftwood stick protruded its point through
the reedy edge of the path. Upheaving the stick, he
grasped it firmly, parted the reeds and peering through
them scanned the whole inlet closely for signs of friend
or foe. Softly the sedges sighed as they moved in a
rhythmic tidal pattern.

Despite a sense of increasing danger the boy continued on the path. "On the island," thought he, "is a
pirates' cave, and the marsh conceals their treasure."
He began to rehearse the reply he would make to the
townsmen of Eastham Parish when they gave him ten
bright pieces of gold in reward for slaying the pirates.

"I thankee, good sirs," said Jeremy Snow, bowing
down to a cattail plume, "for the honor ye do me, and
for the fine gift of the ten pieces of gold. But I have
treasure enough to buy me a palace in London Town.
So I would ye should give the gold to the poor in the
name of my brave little dog who was lost, lured into a
pirates' lair."

Despite the righteous tone of this speech it lacked
a suitable flourish. Jeremy brought his brows together,
in the throes of an elegant art — but he never lost
sight of the prints on the path, or ceased to track them
closely.

"Goodmen," said he, "since thus ye insist, I will
tell ye how I slew them. Alone I stood with my back
to the reeds, and I called aloud to the pirates: 'Come
forth, ye rogues, ye foul sea devils! Come forth to
single combat!'

"Then one by one they came out of the cave, and the first was an Indies man, with a scarlet cloth bound round his head. Bull rings hung in his dragged-down ears, and he carried a long curved knife. I knocked the knife up! It fell on the path. Stooping, I seized it and with his own blade I slew that Indies pirate!

"The next came creeping up through the sedge with a Spanish dagger in his teeth. He sought to spring at me from the rear but I whirled in my tracks and with my staff I smote him a blow like a harpooneer. He rolled from the bar to the bogwater and sank with a deefening howl."

Jeremy's powers flagged. So he skipped the account of the following five to describe the death of the Captain.

"At last he came forth — the Pirate King — with a powdered wig on his head. With a tricorn hat and a gold button coat and dangling lace at his sleeve. He tested the rapier in his hand. 'Boy,' said he, 'ye are made of stern stuff. Will ye join my pirate crew?'

" 'Look about ye, pirate,' I answered him coldly, 'how dead men clutter my path. Look on their faces, Sea Robber King! Behold your pirate crew!' "

The battle waged for a day and a night, then faded before a new vision. A princess arose from the Golden Marsh. On the top of her head she wore a bright crown. Her apron was broidered with rubies and pearls and she held a mill-flour cake in her hand coated with smooth-sticky sirupy paste made out of Indies sugar.

'Prince,' said she, 'for twenty long years I have been chained in yon cave. My father,' said she, 'is the Spanish King and I am heir to his throne. So if ye will wed me, Prince Florizel, ye shall rule the Spanish Main."

She divided the mill-flour cake in half and they sat in the sand and ate it.

Filled as he was with this vision of life, Jeremy's clear Cape-canny eyes yet saw at a glance a place ahead where a soft light reflected upward beyond new-parted reeds.

" 'Tis a corpse light over a Glory Hole!" he thought, and shivered with joy. He crept on silent feet toward the place, then pushed the tall reeds wider apart and peered into a pool of swampwater.

Clear it shone, as if lighted within, as the sun's rays filtered through it, and on the marshbottom a lobster swayed. A pair of rusty iron spectacles lay on the sand beside him. In front of the lobster was an open log-book into which he gazed for all the world as if he were reading its pages.

The lobster lifted his head. A deep bass voice welled up from below, saying "Boy, *one;* Boy, *white.*"

At the sound, the hero, Prince Florizel, slayer of countless pirates, found that his knees gave way beneath him and he slowly sank on the sand.

"Ods me," he muttered, "landlubbers speak true when they say this marsh is quare. There be goings-on in here," he added, "that be not quicksands only!"

"Go along, go along," boomed a froggy voice. He drew up his knees and with hands clasped around them

pulled them back to their senses. Then he tried to
think calmly, clearly. Failing of this, like wiser men
he strengthened his mind with an image — his father's
vessel, the *Abigail,* alone on the wide, wide waters,
moving by the chart of stars.

He rose and set forth once more. The footprints
and paw prints continued. The hidden path turned
and twisted. High reeds hid from view the dark island,
the sunny mainland, the way before and behind him.
So he did not perceive until some time later, when he
smelled the spicy tang of it, that a thick bank of fog
was drifting in from the sea and the outer beach.

After a period of anxious tracking he came up
against a barrier: the sand bar disappeared entirely
under a pool of water.

"There be naught to do but wade it," thought Jeremy, grateful that the water was clear.

Before entering the pool he called loudly, "Bimini!
Bimini!" He also called Long John. No answer
echoed over the marsh, but as if in response to his
shouts, the surface of the poolwater was broken by a
sleek brown head with ears flat back and an evil-look-
ing water rat swam about in the center of the pool. It
regarded him closely with beady eyes, leaving behind,
as it moved through the ripples, a prow-shaped silver
wake.

"How Bimini would go for him," thought Jeremy,
and he brought down his stick on the surface of the
pool with a loud splashy slap. The rat remained in the
center of the pool and showed two yellow fangs.

"I suppose," said Jeremy crossly to the rat, "ye have not set eyes on a little Scots dog? If ye had, ye wouldn't be here!"

"Boy, be not sure," said a squeaky voice followed by an ugly little laugh which made Jeremy's blood run cold.

The pool would make anyone's blood run cold. Its icy transparent water began to numb his feet. He waded deeper and deeper, heading for the opposite shore. As he neared the center of the pond, the rat swerved away from him and he was glad when he crossed center safely and the height of the water fell.

Before he reached the land ahead he paused to survey its beach. In the April sun the sand looked warm but on it there were no footprints. He had, then, lost the hidden path and must continue to wade round the pool. Perhaps he should warm his feet, he thought, on the sun-bright welcoming sand. He took a quick step forward. Then he was falling, falling. There was no land, no water, no sky, only a horrible sucking hole through which he plummeted down. He tried to hurl his body backward. He kept his head and twisted as he fell, full length and sidewise, at an angle such that he succeeded in thrusting the point of his stick in the solid ground behind him. The ground was covered by poolwater. Nevertheless he rolled back into it, gasping for breath and gulping down huge throatfuls of saltwater.

When once again the pool bottom felt solid beneath him, he rose to his feet, dripping wet, shook himself, rubbed his eyes and reached for his cobblered shoes. His shoes were gone! He clutched for them wildly all around his neck. He stared at the shore and the pool-water. Then patiently he stood and waited, chilled by the shivery April wind, waited gravely, anxiously for the churned water to clear.

Gradually the sandy soil sank back to the bottom of the pool. Avoiding any forward move, Jeremy carefully poked the poolbottom with the end of his driftwood stick. Without a doubt his shoes were gone, quickmired, lost forever. "What ever shall I do?" he thought. "Not enough switchings are possible to atone for such a folly!"

He noticed the leering water rat and was suddenly filled with anger. "So you think we won't get you, Bimini and I?" he jeered, and feeling a stone underfoot, he reached for it and threw it directly at the rat.

The rat disappeared in a whirl of eddies. Jeremy reached for another stone. Taking a shot at the rat somehow seemed to relieve his mind. The rat did not reappear in the pool, but Jeremy's eye caught a quick, low movement far to the right on shore. Something gray-brown slunk into the reeds. " 'Tis the hidden path!" Jeremy turned and surged through the water eagerly. Knee-high, waist-high, almost shoulder-high it came.

He struggled out of his sea jacket and tied the soggy sleeves of it tightly under his chin, hoping to bear the weight of wet wool like an Indian pack on his shoulders. He was a strong swimmer for his age and had no fear of deep water. He took his bearings carefully. On the shore where the rat had disappeared, there were clear traces of trail-breaking. The broken reeds on the edge of the pool formed a matted pattern.

He set forth using the long side strokes with which Cape boys are taught to swim, but as he neared the center of the pool, he smelled the soft sea-flower scent of Cape fogs in spring. A white mist was rapidly blanketing the reeds that rimmed the pool.

Now he must swim for his life. There would soon be no way in which he might peer ahead at the pattern of reeds, no chance to size up the treacherous sand before he left, for its hidden dangers, the safe buoyancy of water. Perhaps there would be no finding of shore if the fog closed down completely. Then Aunt Samantha would be sorry. She might not feel so strongly the loss of the cobblered shoes.

He checked his course across the pool and noted, like the true son of a sailor, that the line of it cut directly across the wind ripples on the surface. With a quivering sigh he discarded the soggy weight of his greatcoat and swam with skill and speed. While the breeze lasted he might be able roughly to hold his direction, but when spring fogs settle over Cape pools, the wind dies quickly down.

Fortune favored him. The fog turned into an up-shetting, down-shetting mist, and when he found his shoreward footing it was on solid sand. He recognized through drifting cloud eddies the matted pattern of broken reeds where the rat had gone ashore. Nevertheless, he tested cautiously every forward move, until he caught a glimpse in the sand of a moccasin print overstepped by the mark of a small paw.

"Here they be!" he shouted joyously, as if he had already found them, and he called aloud. "Bimini! Bimini!" and he called to Long John.

The white mist deepened. He could see no signs of the dark island, no trace of the Dune Land behind him. The echo of his voice came back to him, a hollow ghostly sound.

The great effort of swimming in howdy clothes, following as it had the terrible moment of struggle to escape from treachery sands, had warmed his blood and taken away the feeling of numbness and cold. But gradually as he hurried along on a clearly marked trail that led from the pool, he became aware of the chill of the wind that was cruelly biting his back. His teeth chattered. Numbness like that brought on by wading crept up his arms and legs.

He plodded forward at a steady pace. "Surely Mistress Hallett will help me," he thought. "She was a good friend of my mother's. She is our cousin to boot. Perhaps she will know about Long John, and will let me dry by her fire."

The path continued to turn and twist. After a while, despite the fog he could tell that the reeds were thinning, that the bar was approaching shore.

"Ahoy, Mistress Hallett!" he called. "Ahoy! I seek your aid!"

A clear voice answered him, a young, brisk voice with a ringing tone. "Jeremy!" the voice called clearly.

Through the mist a whiter mist came hurling. It flung itself against Jeremy's body with an unmistakable, furry impact. Jeremy clasped it in his arms. "Bimini," he whispered, "Bimini!" and tried to put his cheek down on the dog's squirming head. Bimini wriggled, sniffed, whimpered. He stuck his head tight into Jeremy's neck. He licked the boy's face and barked.

He barked —

"Who called me?" queried Jeremy. Holding Bimini tight in his arms, he cried aloud, *"Who called?"*

"I called, master," said Bimini, but all the sound that Jeremy heard was a short bark that ended in a low dismal growl. For Bimini's eyes no longer held the look of one enchanted. At the first touch of his master's arms, the spell of the Sea Witch broke.

He had failed to save the *Abigail*. He had failed to get warning to Jeremy. The smoke signal had risen at dawn; the *Abigail* sailed to her fate. He could not bring to this boy that he served tidings of the hazardous seas through which his father sailed. For a moment he drooped in Jeremy's arms. Then, because he was only a dog, and because his master came, the past lost much of its shadow, the future blurred to a dream, his heart flamed high with loyalty and time stood still for joy.

2

The Boy and Maria

"Ahoy, Mistress Hallett!" called Jeremy. "Ahoy! I seek your aid!" From a distance a woman's voice came thinly: "Where away? Where away?"

"Here by the hidden path," cried Jeremy. "I dare not climb the shore."

"All's well on the landward beach," replied the voice. "Wait by the high rock."

Jeremy put Bimini down on the lower slope of the sand. The dog ran ahead, then growled and yapped and leaped about in the mist.

"What ails ye?" Jeremy's voice was sharp with puzzlement and foreboding. Bimini whisked back to him.

jumped against him, then darted forward. Jeremy
groped his way upslope. The mist was rapidly thickening. He almost stumbled over his dog, who was engaged, he discovered, in a lively mock battle with a
giant uncoiled snake, a terrible python of a snake
larger in size, different in marking, from any snake
Jeremy had ever seen in the bogs and marshes of the
Dune Country.

"On guard!" he cried, but Bimini continued to war-
whoop and to caper. Drawing hesitantly nearer,
Jeremy peered through the fog: the snake was dead —
had been dead some time. He cast a quizzical glance
at Bimini, who was now seated on the sand beside
him, with a cock of the head and a general air like that
of a conqueror king.

"The way you act," said Jeremy, "one would think
you had killed that snake yourself." Bimini looked up
gravely.

The two continued to mount the beach, the dog
close at his master's heel. A high dark rock loomed
out of the mist. Over its ledge protruded the head of
an ancient snapping turtle. Keeping at respectful distance, Jeremy waited by the rock. The fog, now thicker
than ever, was seeping through his wet clothes. Its
clammy fingers stroked his spine. He could scarcely
see Bimini, though he felt the warmth of the dog's
body pressing close against him.

The blurry light of a lantern appeared, moving toward the rock. A pleasant voice called, "Who bespeaks me?"

"I, Jeremy Snow."

"What brings you here, young Jeremy?"

"My dog — he was lost. And I — quickmired. Then the fog came down."

"How did you know the way to the Island?"

"I followed Long John's trail."

The lantern approached more closely through the mist. It was raised slowly till its light shone full on Jeremy's face. Of the Witch he could see nothing save a long dark cloak that merged into fog, and a pointed hood, and now and again the lantern-shine of her eyes.

The lantern wavered, was lowered quickly. A soft voice whispered, "Abigail!"

"She was my mother," said Jeremy.

"You be very like her," replied the Witch. She took his cold hand in her warm, soft hand, to guide him through the pine-tree path.

"Mistress Hallett," said Jeremy. "We on the mainland are seeking news of Long John."

"Long John keeps watch at the Outer Point. The seas are rising with the full moon tides. A great storm is brewing."

"He is wont to stay in our summer kitchen when the winds blow high."

"The town fathers bade him serve again as Coast Watcher tonight. If the seawater breaks through the sand barriers, as it did some twenty year ago, it will drown the lowland farms."

"He does not always come to us," said Jeremy, "but then we see the light in his window. Last night there was no candle."

"The full of the tides will pass tonight. Long John will return to the Island soon for food and warmth. After you have dried out by my fire, he will take you safely home."

"Thankee, Mistress Hallett," said Jeremy. "My mother loved you well."

"We were young together," said the Sea Witch. "Alas, we were young together — " Her voice dropped, faded. She was silent. Fog encircled them. Jeremy, holding her smooth-fingered hand, felt mist sting the lids of his eyes.

Bimini, unwontedly silent, followed close at his heel.

"My dog, Mistress Hallett," ventured Jeremy, "will he be safe inside your house? I have heerd tell there's a wolf there."

"He will be safe. Wu Wang is tamed and his eyes are partly blinded. He does not move about any more and of late he does not eat."

"I am not affrighted for myself," said Jeremy, which was not true, but he needed to say it to give a renewing strength to his will, for now through the thick and clouded air he made out the shadow of a tiny house with winking brightly lighted windows, and, by the turning of the bones within him, he knew this was the house of a witch.

"Will Long John be soon in the coming? I would not trouble you overmuch." He spoke with a hesitant voice.

"Jeremy," said the Sea Witch gently, " 'twas your mother who stood alone at my side when the townsmen stoned me away. 'Tis your father who brings me food and takes my woven cloth for selling. You are twice welcome to my hearth."

Jeremy thanked Mistress Hallett. Whenever she spoke his mother's name something caught at his breath. His father and Aunt Samantha seldom talked of the past. Jeremy had learned not to question them for he saw that remembrance of his mother's loss beset their hearts too sorely. He recalled that this same breathlessness, this sundered, lonely feeling, had come upon him once before, as he stood at the edge of the Golden Marsh when the reeds and the waters sighed to him, and the ripples sang, "Lost, lost."

"The power of the Sea Witch moves within me. I must be wary," he thought.

Inside the house on the Secret Island a hearthfire burned brightly. A drip-torch shone on a table by the settle. Two candles flickered at the two front windows. The room seemed warm and bright.

As Mistress Hallett stepped across the doorstone, she flung back the hood of her cloak. Then Jeremy saw her

golden hair and the sea-blue depths of her eyes. He
also saw a great gray wolf who turned on them a vacant
gaze, following with its pale, sad eyes the movements
of its mistress, yet lying like a figure of stone beside
the glowing hearth.

"Now for some hot Jamaica tea!" Maria Hallett,
brisk in manner, seemed far from a moon-begotten
witch or the daughter of a pirate king. In fact, so *very*
like Aunt Samantha that Jeremy felt his fears were
groundless. He loathed Jamaica Tea!

It always went with a wetting. To no avail he had
argued and pleaded with Aunt Samantha and his
father. Prudently now he made no comment. Better
not argue with a witch.

She disappeared into the upstep bedroom and reappeared with a huge pair of sailorman's bellbottom
trousers and a warm bide-away shawl. "These be a
mite too big," said she smiling at the long-legged trousers. "Bundle into them as best ye can until your
clothes are dry."

She inspected him more closely.

"Have you no shoes, Jeremy?"

"They are lost in the quicksand, Mistress Hallett."

"Have you no sea jacket either?"

"Alas," said Jeremy, "I could not swim with it. I
cast it away in the pool."

"It does not matter," said Mistress Hallett. "We
shall find them again shortly."

This was a very unlikely thought. Jeremy glanced

at his mother's friend. She had no look of evil.

"Dry yourself by the fire," she ordered. "Tie the trousers round you with this braid of wool, while I search a chest in my bedroom. I have a present for you there."

She put a copper kettle on the fire, then disappeared into a downstep room where the light of a candle flickered up, and Jeremy heard her moving. The wolf on the hearth did not stir.

The boy pulled off his clammy shirt and his heavy water-soaked trousers. He hauled the bellbottoms up to his waist, and tied their folds around him with the stout braid of wool. He wrapped his shoulders in the bide-away shawl, and when Mistress Hallett returned, was engaged in trying to roll the trouser legs up over his feet to his ankles. He prayed that they would stay rolled up, for he must be able to walk about, and if need be, to run.

"Sit here, on the settle," said Maria Hallett, "while I brew some ginger tea."

She brewed it just as Aunt Samantha brewed it and poured him a steaming cup. As soon as its burning spice could be swallowed, he gulped it quickly down, being full of care that as he drank he did not make any faces.

Seated opposite him by the table, her fair hair lighted by the drip-torch glow, Mistress Hallett leaned toward him and smiled.

"'Tis not so hard as ye think, Jeremy. Your mother

and I, we drank it oft. Your mother hated it, too."

"I am grateful for its warmth," said Jeremy, for he felt a comfortable heat inside him, and his hands and feet were growing warm and the chills had left his spine.

Bimini kept close to his feet, even here, across-hearth from a wolf. The dog made no move to attract attention, which was not like him at all. Jeremy wondered: Was Bimini afeered? Of the wolf? Of the Witch? Of the coming storm? Of even the dark little house itself hidden away completely in the thick pine forests of the island?

After ginger tea was safely swallowed, Mistress Hallett took from her pocket a small oval circle, backed with engraven gold. In the circle was the portrait of a woman with curling brown hair and shining blue eyes and a small, pointed chin.

"Look, Jeremy," said Maria Hallett. "This is a likeness of your mother. When we were young, each of us had a locket-piece made for t'other. Mine I have saved for *you*."

Jeremy made no move to take the locket from her hand.

"Mistress Hallett," he said in a piteous voice, revealing all his doubts and fears, "in this ye surely would not bespell me? Is it my mother's face?"

"Aye, Jeremy. Fair she was, but her beauty no portrait can discover, for it was in the quick turns of her mind, the sun and shadow that graced her."

Jeremy felt strangely shy of the picture. Portraits were rare in the New Colony and a locket-likeness, or miniature, was something of which he had never heard. There had been no record in the house by the dunes of his young mother's face.

"Take it in your hand," said Maria Hallett. "It belongs, now, to you."

Jeremy took the locket. He held it tightly in hands that were hot. He was frightened that he would drop it, or by some evil fortune destroy it. He wanted to look at it all alone, long and alone, long and alone. He wanted to show it to his father.

Maria Hallett watched him curiously. With the bide-away shawl wrapped round his shoulders and his brown hair tousled as it dried by the fire, he did not know that he closely resembled the picture in his hand. So like was he, that from Maria the years dropped away like spring snow at Sun-up, and memories long laid aside came creeping back to her heart.

The moment of quiet was broken by a sharp knock on the door. For Mistress Hallett the knock was familiar, since she did not turn her head as she called, "Enter, my brother. Enter."

Long John stood in the doorway, his tall body straight as an arrow. Pools of water dropped on the doorstone from the edges of his deerskin coat.

"Broken are the sands," he said briefly. "The Island floats in seawater. I go to warn the shore."

If he saw Jeremy, he gave no sign of it.

"Long John! Long John! I must go with ye now!"
Jeremy sprang up from the settle.

"You should not have come. 'Tis too late to return."

"I will swim beside you," said Jeremy.

"The tides will outswim you, little Brother."

"Then I will hold to your coat, Long John."

"And drown us both in the tidewater."

"Jeremy," said Mistress Hallett, "once before a
spring storm broke through the sands. There is nothing to fear on this island. The waters will rise around
us, but my house stands high in the center. We shall
be safe here together."

"I will bear word to your grandaunt," said Long
John. "When the storm falls silent, when the tides
turn, when the water dies down in the marshes, then
you and I together, little Brother, will swim through
the Green Pool."

"I must go *now*," said Jeremy. "Aunt Samantha is
all alone."

"She will be safe in the Dune Country. 'Tis a short
storm coming, a *trapado*." Long John continued as if
speaking to himself, half prophecy, half musing: "It
will blow from the land for half the night. There will
be a small hole in the center. Then the winds will
fiercely blow from the sea. Afterward comes a great
stillness and the sun will flower at dawn."

"Jeremy," said Mistress Hallett. "Will ye not stay,
as long ago your mother stayed with me through storm?

The seas will swirl about us. The trees will twist and
the heavens cry out. I have been lonely through many
storms. Will ye not bide with me, now?"

Jeremy felt strangely grown. "Tell Aunt Samantha," he said to Long John, "that I came to find my
dog. Tell her I meant no wrong."

Long John's lip turned up at the corner.

"She will find that a worth-nothing reason. She will
say you broke your word."

"Would that my father were home from sea!" The
heartfelt wish burst from Jeremy's lips. "I bide but
poorly with women!"

*   *   *

After a supper of kettle-brew and dried berries pot-
boiled on the fire, Maria Hallett led Jeremy into the
upstep bedroom. His shirt had dried. He put it on
thankfully and crawled under the beautiful woven
coverlet on the bed. The work of Mistress Hallett's
loom, a pattern of stars on a blue ground, it was very
unlike the "repeater" designs of the women of Eastham Parish.

"Jeremy," asked Maria Hallett, "shall we leave your
candle burning, to light you into slumber? 'Tis an un-
familiar room you are in and a long day you have
lived." She kissed him gently on the lips, touched
Bimini's head with her hand, and went quickly out of
the room.

He wondered whether or not she knew that that

was his first kiss. Aunt Samantha called it a tavern
practice to be resisted by all young Peninsula men who
expected to follow the sea. Yet how pleasant it seemed
when the heavens were dark with the sound and fury
of approaching storm, and the mind grew timorous
and solemn before the long, long night.

Bimini lay close. She could not be a real witch,
thought Jeremy, or the dog would not have licked her
hand. He hugged Bimini tightly. He looked at the
strange coverlet. Big stars and little stars were woven
into it, the North Star, the Bear, the Hunter with his
wondrous jeweled belt. These were the constellations
by which his father sailed. The sky itself Mistress Hallett had chosen for the pattern that lay over him. This
knowledge calmed his fears. For mariners and sons of
mariners turn to the fixed and measurable stars, in
life's veiled or perilous hours, since over the trackless
waters such peace and order reign.

Drowsily he thought of the marsh and of the fair
Marsh Princess who would make a biddable shipmate
to have, stirring about in the home. By day she could
mix up mill-flour cakes, and he would lick the spoon-
batter. By night in the glow of the low-banked fire
they would wrastle book-larning together — and her
jeweled apron would gleam — gleam like the lid on
the magical chest of which he had caught a tempting
glimpse through the door of the downstep room.

He began to explain to the Princess about the high
dunes by the sea, and his Lookout Ledge, and his fine

sand sled, and his father's fleet-winged sloop. He decided to go on the voyage himself when his father returned her to Spain. As the rightful heir to the Spanish throne he should take a look at the foreign ports and the in-and-out seas that surround them. That was the principal part of a realm and all that he cared to claim.

Perhaps — he paused, for now *she was there,* really there, in her own true self, by the upstep bedroom door. With her golden crown and her tender smile. Silently she came toward him. Her cool hand touched his forehead, and brushed the hair back from his brow. Then she blew out the light of the candle and the room was blotted and gone.

"I will sail away with ye to Spain," he whispered.

And again, as the night came darkly down, *"I will voyage with ye to Spain."*

*   *   *

He was wakened from sleep by Bimini. The storm was lamenting loudly. He could hear a wild fashing of the trees. Bimini, making no sound at all, pulled with his teeth at Jeremy's sleeve. Jeremy sat up in bed, with a gloomy feeling that Sun-up had come before it was rightly due. Further aroused, he saw that the light that seeped into the upstep room was not dawnlight from the window, but torchlight from the greatroom door.

"Hush, Bimini," he whispered. "Lie still. Wait for me here."

Bimini rumbled a protest, but remained upon the bed. Jeremy pushed him under the coverlet and moving slowly, on tiptoe, approached the lighted door. It was half open. Looking through, he saw a faded red glow on the hearth. Wu Wang was lying there sleeping. On the table the drip-torch burned low.

Then he heard voices whispering from the other side of the room. To see this he applied his eye to the narrow crack in the door jamb. Mistress Hallett was seated by a window. She had thrown a bright shawl across her shoulders and was speaking in a low grave tone to a great black bird. A night hawk, it looked, perched on the window ledge, and on its back sat a curious figure, a tiny man with a feathered cap, huge ears and a scarlet reefer.

Jeremy put his ear close to the crack. Answering Mistress Hallett's words, the strange little man was speaking in a voice like a tinkling bell.

"Aye," said the voice, "the *Whidah* rides the storm. She has driven in close to the outer bars, but the spinning-wheel winds waft her seaward."

"What of the *Abigail?*"

"Sunk in the sea! She lies in her deep sea tomb! The Black Bellamy stove in her hull with a blast, a broadside from his great port guns. She sank ere the storm began."

"And Captain Snow?"

"He went down with his ship, and was saved from the sea by the pirates. He lies chained to a block in the slave galley, and suffers from a gash on his head."

"Is it thus," muttered Maria Hallett, "that Sam treats one who befriended me staunchly through the long years of waiting?"

"Captain Snow and the pirate Captain quarreled. Black Bellamy struck the Cape Captain a blow, struck him a blow with his cutlass."

"Struck him in chains?" demanded Maria, her voice harsh and stern.

"Aye," said the strange little man.

Jeremy could stand no more. On legs that shook he stumbled forward.

"Mistress Hallett," he cried, "is it true what he says? Is my father a prisoner of pirates? Is the *Abigail* sunk in the sea?"

The bird flew up from the window ledge, the tiny figure astride of its back. The bright shawl dropped from Maria Hallett and she turned, darted forward, seized Jeremy roughly, shook him hard by the shoulders.

"Wake up!" she commanded. "Wake up, boy. What ails you? Are ye dreaming?"

"No, Mistress Hallett. No!" said Jeremy and he looked her straight in the eyes.

She put her arm about his shoulders, drew him to her, sat down on the settle.

"Be calm, young sailorman," she cautioned. "There is naught to fear. Your father is safe, and the *Abigail* rides the storm."

"How know you this?"

"Hush, Jeremy. You wake from a troubled dream.
I will pour you a draught of elderberry wine. We shall
build up the fire and sit here beside it, and you may
tell me of your dreaming."

Jeremy drank the wine that she gave him. At his
first cry Bimini had come from the bedroom, and the
dog stayed close to his master. Yet Jeremy noted with
wonder that he showed no sign of fear.

"Of what did ye dream?" asked the Sea Witch
gently.

"I did not dream," said Jeremy. "I *beheld* a great
night hawk who perched yonder on the window ledge.
A strange little man rode on his back. The man said
that the *Abigail* was sunk, that my father was prisoner
of the pirates!"

"Dreams are contrarious things," said Maria. "If ye
tell such tarradiddles to Aunt Samantha she will feed
ye wormgall and tree-syrup."

Jeremy's gaze never left her face.

"Mistress Hallett." He addressed her gravely. "I
beseech you to deal with me more in honor — for ye
be in truth a witch."

"And you a strange boy," said Maria Hallett, "past
believing like your mother!"

She threw a pine log on the fire; twice paced the
length of the greatroom; then paused and looked into
Jeremy's eyes with a gaze direct and true.

"Even so," she said, "I *am* a witch, or what you and

the townsmen call a witch for want of some wiser word and a deeper understanding."

"Mistress Hallett," cried Jeremy, "if ye are witch woman, can ye not save my father?"

"Save him?" said she.

"Aye," answered Jeremy. "Have ye not power over ships at sea? Can ye not destroy the *Whidah?*"

"Your father would go down with the ship."

"Can ye not bring him safe to shore? He knows every foot of these northern coasts, the outer bars, the undersea drag, where the beaches are firm, where the path leads up the dune-cliff. If ye will free him and destroy the pirates, *he will escape from the sea.*"

"You do not know what you ask," she said. "'Tis true that I sold my soul for a ship and must pay with a ship for the soul's return. But never in all these terrible years have I been of a will to drown young seamen for the sake of my own salvation."

"But these be blackhearted men," said Jeremy, "sea robbers, doers of evil, who come to burn our homes. Perhaps never again," he pleaded, "will a pirate ship ride in so close to the bars of our own Dune Country. Such men ye *must* destroy!"

"You are son of your father." Maria spoke bitterly. "His words echo on your lips."

"Where is he now?" asked Jeremy. "Alas, where is he now?"

The Sea Witch seemed to be listening no longer. She stared into the fire.

"A ship for a ship," she whispered. "For ten long years I have waited. And now white-winged as the swans of Devon, a ship as fair as the star of evening, laden with ivory and spices and gold brings back my brave, lost lover!"

She laughed, a brief and bitter laughter; turned away from the hearth; from a jeweled chest took a small delicate vial. She threw a few drops from this into the fire which flared like a torch, then the flames grew transparent. In them appeared, as in a mirror, a great ship scudding before the wind with her sails close-furled and her deck gear lashed, and laughter and drinking in her cabin.

The flame died down. Another rose to reveal a prisoner in irons. A blood-soaked sleeve band bound his head. His face was hidden in his arms.

The figure faded. An old man in a black cloak appeared. Unlike the others he looked out from the flame and up toward Jeremy and the Sea Witch. He nodded, bowed, and smiled. In his two hands he held two ships and he seemed to weigh and balance these. One had a golden serpent coiled under her slender bowsprit. One of the ships was the *Whidah* with the plumed bird of paradise for figurehead at her prow.

"Old man," said the Witch, "my soul comes high. 'Tis the fairest ship in Christendom."

Jeremy spoke no word. He sat very still till the flame died down. His hands were clenched; his heart thumped in his chest, for the wounded prisoner he had seen in the flames he knew to be his father.

A clouded brightness returned to the fire. Mistress Hallett spoke to him then. "In the center of the storm," said she quietly, "there comes a lull when the winds die down. The center draws nigh, Jeremy. I must leave you and go forth into it, if I would save your father."

"Is there aught I could do to help?" asked Jeremy.

"Aye," she answered, "tend the hearth while ye wait. Keep the house door barred. If I come not again, open to no other voice than the voice of Long John, or your father."

She pulled a gold ring from her finger and held it in her hand. "Have you," she asked, "by any fair chance, aught that belongs to your father?"

"I have a lucky piece, Spanish bully-ones."

"Give it me, Jeremy, now."

He pulled over his head a string with a holed Spanish coin on it.

"That will do well," said the Sea Witch, "that and my troth ring together." She smiled a rueful, twisted smile. Suddenly Jeremy grieved for her.

"Had my mother lived," said he to her, "she would have taken good care of us. Sorrows would not overwhelm us."

Maria Hallett drew about her the long dark cloak that she had worn when Jeremy first had summoned her. She stood briefly by the hearth.

"The center of the storm has come," she said. "Tonight I go into it to cast such magic as no Cape woman ever has cast before. If I succeed, I shall save your father. If I fail, do not betray me, Jeremy. Upon no account, lest ye shatter the Spell, put foot outside my door."

She took two glowing embers from the hearth and placed these in an iron kettle. Carrying the kettle she opened the door and disappeared into the night.

"Be of good courage," she called back clearly. Her words in their brightness were so like his father's that Jeremy felt tears hot in his eyes and he closed the door in a hurry.

The Book
of
the Pirates

1

The Great Storm

Barnabas Hobb, chartmaker, sat alone in the cabin of
the *Whidah*. The ship rose and fell in the coastal
surge. The top of the water was mirrored smooth as
if wiped with an oily rag. Barnabas pulled from a roll
of charts a neatly lettered coastwise map. He seated
himself at the carved oak table, spread this map full
length before him, bent over to peer at it closely, made
on it a small neat mark.

He was not dressed in fine-fashioned clothes like the
more prosperous pirates, nor in sailorman's garb with
a greased queue and a short sea jacket with a leathern
collar. Nor was he dressed like the Indies Bonniemen

in sash-topped breeks and a bright headcloth woven by
the women of the slave countries. He might have been
a Sussex farmer, or a freeman of the City of Boston, in
his plain gray homespun suit with its white turnover
collar.

Signed on new for this northern voyage he was object of watchful suspicion. Pirates are skittish as colts
in spring when a new hand signs articles, for he may
prove spy or he may turn King's Man or he may be
plotting high thievery. Barnabas Hobb more than
most was subject of gossip and fear.

He was, and this was at root of the gossip, favored
by the Black Bellamy, who night after night would sit
in the cabin studying the chartmaker's maps. Paul
Williams and Leboues, the Frenchman, Sam's most
loyal and able of captains, knew all too well what
transpired in the cabin. Mark on a map a sunken
treasure, be it but an hundredth of the *Whidah's* tak-
ings, or half at best of the rumored cargo of vessels
ranging the seas, and Sam Bellamy's eyes would gleam,
he would plot by the hour schemes of salvage, forget-
ful that any long rendezvous may prove death to a buccaneer. Night after night in the cabin of the *Whidah*
Barnabas played on his folly.

The chartmaker rolled up the map on the table. He
took from his pocket a small worn book in which he
kept ship's tally. One hundred and fifty-eight souls
were listed including the forced men and wounded,
and the prisoners chained in the slave galley. To these
must be added the Cape captain and his sullen crew

fished out of the ocean after their small defiant vessel had been sunk in a rousing fight.

The chartmaker paused, the book open in his hand, as Jan Julian, apprentice pilot, entered the cabin door. Jan was a Cape man of Indian blood and had been summoned by Captain Bellamy to identify such men as he could among the prisoner crew. He was ready to die for the Black Bellamy, whose slightest word was the word of a God, but his impassive and silent ways concealed this fiery allegiance. Barnabas Hobb made much of Jan. He undertook to teach the Indian navigation and charting, and Jan proved an apt pupil though cautious of speech and uneasy.

"Welcome, brother," said the chartmaker pleasantly, addressing the Indian Colony-fashion. "What fish did ye catch with the bait of the guns?"

"Eastham fish," said Jan Julian.

"Know ye their names?"

"Nay, master. None save the Captain whom all men know. He has great renown on the seas."

"Would it, perchance, be Caleb Snow of the Dune Lands in Eastham Parish?"

"Aye, master. But he dies, I fear. He bleeds much from a wound on the head."

"By our cannon volleys or the buffeting seas?"

"Neither," said Jan Julian.

"Whence comes this wound?"

"'Twas brought on by himself. By his evil tongue! By his insolent ways!"

"So Caleb defied the Black Bellamy?"

"Aye, they quarreled and our captain struck him, for he called us sea robbers, black spawn of Lucifer!"

"Well?" said Barnabas Hobb.

"'Tis not true!" Jan Julian's dark eyes blazed. "We be freemen who fight for the right of the weak. We be foes of the English King."

"Was there a woman's name bandied about betwixt these men in their quarrel?"

"I do not know," said Jan Julian, but his black eyes shifted from the chartmaker's gaze and Barnabas nodded and smiled.

He pulled out a drawer in the oak table and took from it a bag of coin.

"Young Jan," said he, "have ye run of the ship?"

"Aye, Master, I pass where I please."

"Then go below to the slave galley. Bespeak each sailor of the Cape vessel. Speak the man fair, but softly. Give to each a coin to seal the bargain and promise of a file to sever his chains, if he will tell ye his name."

"'Tis of no use to waste coin, Master."

"Do as ye are bid," said the chartmaker.

"But these," protested Jan Julian stoutly, "be men too wise to the bluewater to let their true names be writ down in a tally. For then our captain has power to claim them. They may be prisoned in Boston Gaol, haled before Admiralty Court for trial, mayhap condemned as pirates!"

"Do as ye are bid," said Barnabas. His eyes looking

into Jan Julian's were as somber as the Cape Indian's.

The two men broke off their converse as the Captain entered the cabin. He flung himself into a chair by the table, opposite Barnabas Hobb.

"We are approaching Cape Cod," said he. "By relay of signals our consorts draw nigh, to stand by for their sailing orders."

"'Tis high time," said Barnabas Hobb, "to make known the plans for a landing."

Sam ignored Barnabas' words. "I would there were eight in consort," said he, "but the Cape sloop fought us to a finish. Or it might have been said that I sailed to the North in command of a full sea squadron."

Barnabas caught up his mood. "And it may be yet, if our luck holds out. Ye will then be Admiral of the Fleet with a squadron of sail, a King's Pardon, an Emperor's fortune to boot."

Sam's gaze turned ironically to the suave face of the chartmaker, and his mood turned sharply sour.

"Let the facts be clear, Mr. Hobb," said he. "I am in command of a treasure ship with a cargo rich in booty. With a muttering, angry, mutinous crew! With a flock of prize vessels sailing wide but ready like vultures to pounce for a kill, commanded by prizemasters jealous of heart, greedy of gold, hotheaded. And the *Whidah*, the loveliest ship in the world, I must risk on the perilous, shifting bars of the Graveyard of Ships, the Cape Country."

"Why must this be?" asked Jan Julian.

"I dare not give over her helm, my boy, not for a day nor an hour, and I and no other, so I have sworn, must enter at Eastham Sea Gate!"

"Have I not contracted," said Barnabas Hobb, "to bring ye to Eastham shores?"

"'Tis eleven years since the shoals I sighted. What of the wintry sand drifts, Barnabas?"

"The map I made is but two months old, with the readings of leads that I dropped myself on every bar and channel."

"Let me look once again at the chart, Barnabas."

The chartmaker unrolled a map. The two bent over the long oak table to peer at its fine penned numbers.

Still as a cat Jan Julian stood till Bellamy, lifting his head for a moment, encountered the Indian's gaze.

"Jan," said he in a kindly tone, "come, read with us, boy. 'Tis mete ye should learn as a pilot."

Jan Julian approached the table. Slender and young, with muscles of steel, as Sam drew the Indian close to the map, with a hand on the boy's shoulder, Jan's body quivered like a reed in a marsh. Beads of sweat shone on his forelip.

"Captain," said Jan in a soft, shy voice, "there be strange birds winging the air."

"Aye," said Sam, "from the south they come, driven upcoast by the storm."

Jan seemed to gather new courage for speech. "'Tis a spinning-wheel storm," he murmured softly, "spun on the looms of the witches. Were we not wiser to seek quick harbor, or set course for the open sea?"

"We shall soon ride safely in harbor, my boy" — Barnabas spoke with a confident smile — "ere the spinning-wheel storm overtake us."

The Indian put his slender brown finger on the mark new made on the map.

"What reads this sign?" asked he. "'Tis neither bar nor channel here but a barren beach under a high sea cliff where the dunes mount upward and mix their crests with the tall Clay Pounds to the north."

Barnabas peered at the map closely. "Yonder is mark of a treasure." The Indian eyed him intently, then averted his gaze from the chart.

Aloft in the rigging the wind awoke and it thrummed the spinning-wheel tune.

"Hearken!" said Sam, his head lifted. "'Tis the rim of the wheel passes over us now. 'Tis the voice of a great *trapado*."

"A mewling sound," said Barnabas Hobb.

"Alack!" Jan Julian's shy young voice took on prophetic tone. "Masters," he pleaded, "hear me, I pray. Send a sloop of light burden through Eastham Sea Gate if ye must enter the Cape Country. Spread the *Whidah's* wings to the offshore winds. Let them bear her away to the wide sea reaches to breast this spinning-wheel storm."

"Since when," said Barnabas Hobb coldly, "has a

brown-bodied boy with the blood of Cain set the course of our captain's fleet?"

*   *   *

Far away, in the tropic seas the golden galleons and caravels sleep in their green, translucent tombs. Outworn, outsailed, stabbed to the death by the sharp-nosed, quick-bodied ships of the North, the bones of the lost Armadas stir as the brooding sun draws a fiery mist up into the lower sky. The air sucks upward. The sobbing winds, drawn by the roundabout spin of the earth, whirl at the hub of a disclike wheel — a seething cauldron — a witches' brew — round the eye of the fierce *trapado*.

Power lies dark at the center of the wheel, the wheeling earth and the spinning loom, and the hurricane over the sea. Slowly northward the whirlwind moves, the giant circle of mutinous wind; and again and again, whenever it comes, in terror the small craft flee. And the sharp-nosed, sharklike ships of the north, close-hauled, tight-reefed, turn their prows to the blast, stripped lean to weather a gale.

*   *   *

Sam, with a sea lantern in his hand, descended to the slave galley of the *Whidah*. The air was foul with the fetid smells of bodily illness, sweat, stale food and bilge-water. The prisoners, chained to slave blocks, stirred, and muttered, and groaned. The Captain lifted the shutter of his lantern and directed its rays on man after man, but he kept his own face in shadow, out of the angle of light. On either side of the focus of the lantern men's eyes gleamed like cat's.

How readily, thought Sam Bellamy, darkness turns us into beasts.

The *Whidah* strained heavily, breasted a wave, then pitched and rolled with a stately scroll-like turn. Sam Bellamy staggered. As he righted himself, the swaying lantern cast a faint light on his stern face but the eyes that could blaze and flash and glow now showed no flicker of pity or anger in response to the jarring laughs and threats that greeted his momentary stumble.

The dark lantern paused at length before a prone figure, the face hidden in crooked arms, a blood-soaked bandage on the head.

"Wake, Caleb Snow!" commanded Sam Bellamy.

The figure did not stir, but a faint tensing of the body muscles suggested to Sam that Caleb Snow was neither asleep nor unconscious.

"Caleb," said he, "for the sake of your men, hearken now to me."

Slowly Caleb Snow pulled himself up on one elbow. The heavy chains that bound his legs clanked and dragged on the planking.

"Whatever of evil your damned soul plots, I'll have no part of it!" said he.

"Caleb, no sailing master alive knows these northern coasts as ye do. How many crew of the *Abigail* lie here, rescued from the drowning?"

"All save two," answered Captain Snow wearily, "the mate and the ship's boy."

"It lies within your power, Caleb, to save these prisoned men."

Caleb Snow made no answer. He lifted his head and became aware of the straining of the ship's timbers. The shipmaster in him wakened. He noted the curious way in which the great vessel veered and yawed, for as the seas smote her, though helmed to the wind, she forsook her course and seemed to be drawn by some vast, invisible lodestone accountable neither to wind nor wave and beyond the power of the helm.

"Do ye hear what I hear, Caleb?" Sam Bellamy stood as if bound by a spell, his ear tuned to the sounding gale. "Never have I known storm such as this, yet through its fiercest onset the *Whidah* rode steadfast as a star. Now in the lull, in the eye of the storm, though the winds less fiercely beset her, she plunges through the darksome night as if her sails were spread."

A vast wave battered the *Whidah*. Her captain, his shoulders braced against the low crossbeam of the galley, was almost thrown to the planks.

"What course have we sailed," asked Caleb Snow, "since I bided here in the galley? I am without all knowledge of time. Neither awake nor asleep have I been, but as one who attends God's Judgment."

"Since the *Abigail* sank we have followed the coast up the old southerly searoad. If the lowering skies should lift again, between these terrible walls of water, could ye pilot us into some harbor, Caleb, hidden by the tall cliffs?"

Caleb Snow laughed. "Sam," said he, "only a fool and a braggart would strike a man thus manacled. Now would ye give to the prisoner in chains power to destroy your vessel?"

"No master lives," answered Sam stubbornly, "who would sink the *Paradise Bird.*"

Caleb drew his manacled hands across the blood soaked bandage on his head. "Aye, ye speak true," he admitted.

"Caleb," Sam spoke more persuasively, "freedom I offer, freedom and gold, and a safe harbor for you and your men, if ye will pilot the *Whidah* off these long and terrible reefs that draw her, chained and unresisting, like a moon drawing the tides."

Caleb's lip curled. "Whose word," said he, "have I for this? Ask Maria Hallett of Eastham!"

Sam started as if he were struck. He turned to leave the galley, then wheeled and spoke more gently. "Caleb," he pleaded, " 'tis a fair ship, the fairest ship on the Seven Seas — the 'Paradise Bird' — the *Whidah.*"

Captain Snow again passed his bound hands across his forehead.

"Unchain me, Sam," he ordered. His voice had lost

its blurred thickness, though he still clung dizzily for support to the crossbeam of the galley. " 'Tis not for gold nor freedom I come, though I like freedom well. But a man must fight against rising seas and the lashing heavens that would destroy us, whether the Lord or Satan's Self ride on the wings of storm."

Sam Bellamy took from his pocket a heavy dark key. With this he unlocked the chains that bound Caleb, and sprung the lock on the manacled wrists. As he worked the *Whidah* veered widely, lurching from side to side with a motion like the swing of a clock's pendulum strung to an unseen star.

"I have never," muttered Caleb Snow, "felt ship move thus freely when the course is held to the wind. Are ye sure of the power of your helmsmen, Sam?"

"Come abovedeck," answered Bellamy.

The two made their way upladder till they reached the storm-lashed deck. Clinging to ropes they fought their way aft. Huge combers had driven the taveril in and broke upon the poop. Seamen, hurled from the wheel and the rigging, clung to the wave-washed nets.

At a nod from Bellamy Caleb Snow took the fore spokes of the wheel, with a helmsman muscled like Hercules to hold her true to his bidding. Ice-cold winds battered the storm canvas lashed to protect the wheel deck, yet the helmsman's brow was beaded with sweat and the wheel seemed locked in his fingers.

Then for a few awesome moments the wind died down completely. Caleb, whose strength was failing from loss of blood and long hours of suffering, yet held the *Whidah* to her course. During this lull the clouds lifted. "The center of the storm is passing," warned Sam. "Beware as the winds come about!"

As he spoke, to landward dark vapors were sundered. The rays of the moon that shone high in the sky beat white on a landward cliff. And over the shoals of the hidden bars the salt waves seethed and boiled.

The lone voice of the watch cried out: *Breakers! Breakers ahead!* The words were echoed the whole ship over, cried aloud in the high-pitched wailing tones of seamen whose voices are wont to be raised to outstrip the voice of the gale.

In that brief time of slackened winds and lifting clouds and breakers off the bow, Caleb Snow made out to his wonder, and with a pang of sharp foreboding, the high sand cliffs of the Dune Country and looming over the top of these the Dune Before the Sea.

"Let go anchor!" he ordered. At a nod from Captain Bellamy the great anchor was lowered. It dragged along the sandy sea bottom and the *Whidah* scarce seemed aware of its pull as she moved in a tranced, relentless drift toward the close-walled horizon, toward a line where the black-bodied sea was capped with a long white maelstrom of foam.

There was only one chance and the Cape Captain knew it. No ship could ride while this strange power drove her. In the brief lull at the eye of the storm she must be sheeted and tacked. So he ordered the men to cut her cables and to work her off the coast.

Eagerly, with returning courage, the sailors flew to the yards, their cutlasses out to whip at the gaskets until the huge mainsail lashed itself free and beat like the wings of a giant bird against the straining mast. By a mighty effort the sail was bitted. The *Whidah* lurched. Her wet sides wallowed in a deep wave trough that sought to engulf her. But ever she climbed its surging wall, to windward fought and to windward held, as the eye passed onward into the night, and winds blew from the opposite quarter.

Caleb Snow's strength was soon spent but he had the feel of the ship in his hands, so he tendered the helm to a steel-bodied boy, Jan Julian, the Indian. For a long half-watch Sam and Caleb fought for the *Whidah's* life. Shoulder to shoulder in the canvas-lashed wheelhouse, they held her steadily to the wind but she could not draw ahead. Never free from the menace of foam-capped bars, they kept her bowsprit into the storm but ever a strange tidal magnet drew her back toward the coast.

"Caleb," said Sam, "have ye ever seen ship that handled so in a *trapado?* What is this power that does not yield to a set course and a steady wheel? Her sails belly out till the canvas nigh bursts yet she does not draw ahead!"

A sailor replaced the blood-soaked bandage that bound Captain Snow's forehead. The wound on his temple had ceased to bleed. He had forgotten, as a sailorman will, all problems of human perplexity, all matters of guilt or sin: Sam's crimes as a sea robber; the wrongs Sam had done to Maria; the flag at the vessel's mast. She was a fair and gallant ship fighting against her doom.

"Sam," he said, "if I were a landsman, I should say the *Whidah* was bewitched. I hold not with these tales of sorcery, yet never has ship so strangely failed to answer to her course."

Jan Julian's somber eyes flared. "I have known it this half-watch!" he cried. "We are doomed men, I tell ye! 'Tis the work of the Eastham Witch!"

"Ye lie!" Sam Bellamy's quarterdeck voice outroared the raging storm. He struck down Jan Julian and seized the wheel himself.

"Sam," said Caleb, "beware lest the Indian carry this tale to the crew."

The boy stirred, then slumped heavily. Sam Bellamy made no answer. But after a while came a sudden brief lull and Sam spoke in a calmer voice.

"Caleb," he asked, "how fares Maria? In the India seas they say she's a witch with power over ships at sea."

"Maria," answered Caleb, "lives alone in a hut on Doane Island. She was stoned as a witch by the women of Eastham. Much of her time she spends at her loom — weaving strange patterns and fair."

While thus the two captains spoke together high domes of water beset the *Whidah*, "sea volcanoes," the sailors call them, that breaking discharge a spume that seethes like a rain of pelting, fiery ash from stem to stern of a vessel.

"Caleb," Sam boasted, "Maria Hallett will be dowered as a Princess of Spain. Between decks on the *Paradise Bird* lie twenty thousand pounds in doubloons. There be four hundred bags filled with pieces of eight, gold dust, bars of silver and gold. There's a cargo of elephants' teeth in the ship, and indigo, and Jesuits' bark."

"Aye," said Caleb solemnly, "but there be blood on her decks. And never safe harbor ahead, Sam, nor the riding lights of home."

"I do not plunder the poor, Caleb, like the merchants and lords of the land." Sam's voice held a hint of pleading. "Nor have I drowned an English sailor till this northward voyage compelled it. But here in the open roads, Caleb, I dare not let ship pass — lest she betray me to the King's frigates which would block my return to the Indies."

Caleb seemed not to hear. His thoughts had been turned to the brave young mate of his own lost vessel, the *Abigail,* and to the ship's boy, a towheaded greenhorn, ten years old, on his first sea voyage to bring money to a widowed mother. They two slept cold in the April seas. They would never voyage to the Indies.

The seamen who had taken the half-watch were spent and fearful when word passed among them that the *Whidah* was bewitched. With their muscles strained and their heads aching from roar of wind and thunder of waves, they were stricken anew by the

numbing shock of this most terrible fear. Those to
whom word could not be passed observed in their
fellows unaccountable dread and suffered an inward
panic.

When sails are set in a driving storm there is always
a moment of danger for a ship as the old watch is re-
lieved. For the new watch has not found its mettle;
the old watch yields too soon. Eight bells rang out in
the darkness, and while men struggled along the ropes
to relieve their mates, the ship was born leeward by a
wall of water that thrust her before it like a winged
seed in a cataract, like a flake in an avalanche of snow.

The *Whidah* struck on the outer bar. In a tangle of
wreckage her mainmast fell, and men of both watches
were pinned beneath a storm canvas stiff with frozen
spume. These screamed like the raucous cry of gulls
before they plunged down to the sea.

*   *   *

Barnabas Hobb in a long black cloak stood on the
poop of the *Whidah,* close by her black-browed Captain. Caleb Snow struck down by a spar had sunk in
a heavy faint.

Sam turned on Barnabas fiercely. "Ye have dug the
sea grave of the *Whidah!*" he cried.

"Not I — Not I — " Barnabas' voice rose over the
sounds of the gale: *"If ye would learn how the* Whidah
perished, ask the Sea Witch of Eastham!"

A mountain of seething, churning foam swept over
the pulseless vessel. Sam flung Caleb's body across his

shoulders and clung to the useless wheel. The great comber broke and rolled onward. When Sam's eyes cleared of stinging spume, the chartmaker's slender, black-cloaked body had vanished from the *Whidah's* deck.

*   *   *

In less than a falling of the hourglass sands the storm-worn *Whidah,* heavy with guns, turned bottom-up and her decks fell out, and the guns and gold and much of her cargo still lie, so mariners say, beneath the dark hull that may yet be descried at the ebb of the tide on the bar that lies north of the Dune Country.

After she struck but before she perished Bellamy released the prisoners in irons, so Cape men and pirates struggled together in the wild surfwaters of the storm.

One hundred and one bodies washed ashore from the *Whidah.* The long waves hurled them against the cliff, then sucked them back in the undersea wash to hurl them forth once more. Tom Davis, ship's carpenter, kept alive as the sea swept him landward, and Jan Julian's wits revived when the cold waves wakened his body. He seized a piece of the *Whidah's* wreckage, and managed to slide between shattering waves to secure firm footing on a cliff.

Two other men escaped alive from the open decks of the *Whidah:* Captain Caleb Snow borne on the back of Sam Bellamy, pirate. Sam held the slender inert body on his own wide and powerful back and somehow kept them both alive through the surf and the suck-under rollers.

When Sam climbed out of the seawater, he found footing on a narrow ledge already besieged by ankle-deep foam. From the ledge no path afforded to climb to the highlands above. Still carrying Caleb, Sam seated himself against the wet cliff wall. He chafed the wounded man's hands and spoke. Caleb seemed not to answer, but Sam could detect his labored breathing and the heart pounding in his chest.

After a time the Cape captain revived. The waves were lapping his body, which was gently cradled in Sam's arms as if he were holding a child.

"Whereto have we come?" asked Caleb vaguely.

"Better ye had died unknowing," said Sam. "A cliff-locked ledge we are stranded upon and must drown with the rising tide."

Caleb lapsed into slumber and Sam, fearing the numbness of sleep, spoke again in an effort to rouse him.

"Ye fought a good fight for the ship," he said, his voice close to Caleb's ear. "I owe ye a debt till the end of time, and I would ye might live to conquer the sea for ye are a noble sailor."

" 'Tis piteous cold," said Caleb.

Sam tightened his arms round the ailing body.

"Yea, I would ye might live!" he cried aloud. "Though for me it were best the ledge be a trap, and there be no path for climbing. For I be a fool beset by fools — and with masts too tall for my timbers!"

"Hush, Sam." Caleb's voice came faint and thin to his ear. "Ye be man born out of your time, Sam. With

the wily guidance of Good Queen Bess, ye might have
been King of the Sea."

A cold wave crept about their bodies and smote on
Caleb's chest. He was fully roused. He lifted himself
and felt with his hands along the base of the ledge. It
was made, he discovered, out of splintery peat over-
topped with a coating of sand. Then his hand closed
over a small object, and with the familiar feel of it for
a moment tears rose to his eyes. Bestirring himself, he
spoke with a voice into which new hope crept slowly.

"Sam," he said, "there's a pathway cut from this
shelf of peat to the Dune Country. For a space as we
climb we must cling to wood spikes driven deep into
the cliffside. 'Tis my son Jeremy's lookout ledge that
we have been shipwrecked upon."

His hand closed even more tightly over the clumsy
wooden blunderbuss that Jeremy had made as a weapon
of arms with which to protect the Colony coast from
just such pirates as the one who now in stinging darkness and driving storm supported the boy's father in
his arms.

"With loss of blood and sickness," said Sam, "I
dread that you will fall."

He took off his seajacket soaked with water, and
wringing it out as best he might, he tied it under
Caleb's armpits, knotting it firmly at the Cape Captain's back with a knot that a man could hold to.

"You must take the lead," said Sam to Caleb, "and
I'll be close behind ye. As your feet and hands leave
the spikes in the cliff, mine will fall straightway upon

them. If you grow faint again, hold hard and shout. I'll strike ye a blow to rouse ye. If you reel I'll hold by the coat."

" 'Tis but one hand-over-hand," answered Caleb, "then we strike a steep path to the uplands."

The wind had abated but water now curled in churning eddies around their knees, and slowly, with effort and gasping, Caleb pulled himself up the cliff-side. Sam followed, one handhold behind him, protecting Caleb against outward sway with the pressure of his strong dark head. With a final flagging effort, the two weary seamen pulled themselves over the edge of the cliff to a place where the furrowed sands of the Cape yielded a small sand valley dotted with waxberry clumps that loomed green-black in the gray-black sand.

From this valley a narrow path led upward between two long spurs of cliff to the Dune Before the Sea. Pausing at the full blast of the wind, they made their way forward in moments of lull till they reached the top of the dune. Then, exhausted, Caleb fell forward. Sam carried him over the crest of the dune, but the Cape captain was too weak to stand and Sam too wearied to carry him. So Sam scooped out a hollow of sand. Using his soaked coat for a pillow, he laid Caleb into this hollow, protected from the seaward winds and the fiercest onslaughts of rain.

Then Sam knelt down and placed his mouth close to the Cape captain's ear. "I go for aid," said he. "And if I should see ye no more, Caleb — I owe ye a ship — I shall win ye a ship. Ye fought for mine like a brother!"

"We be men of the sea," answered Caleb simply. "But I would ye had not sunk the *Abigail*. She was named for my young, dead wife."

The night was all dark. Sam could not see at an arm's length before him. But even after so long an absence, he knew that this was the Dune Country, and well he remembered an inlet of tides curving into a golden marsh. If he could but find the edge of this marsh, he might, he decided, follow the path through which, so many long years ago, Maria Hallett had led him. He did not know that Caleb's house was less than a mile from the dune where he stood; and Samantha, fearful of hurricane winds, had doused all lights within it.

Even in darkness and veer-about storms a ship's captain carries the points of the compass inside his head, along with a knowledge of the nature of wind, its tang on the lips, the feel of its blast as it blows from the four quarters. So Sam set out in a southerly direction to find the Golden Marsh. If he thought at all of this as a home-coming to Maria Hallett of Eastham, the exhaustion of his body, the loss of his ship had swept from his mind all purpose. For what seemed immeasurable time he went forward, stumbling, lurching as a spent man moves who has set him a hopeless task to do and has forgotten its meaning.

Suddenly a body of darkness loomed in the night

before him which, had he not been traversing dunes, he might have mistaken for a tree.

Against the wailing of the offsea winds a deep, strong voice bespoke him.

"Hail, brother!"

"Belay, Indian!"

"Whence come you, brother, in the storm?"

"Shipwrecked I be," shouted Sam Bellamy. "There be an hundred like me!"

"Where away wrecked?"

"To the north, Indian."

"What name, sailor?"

"A sea captain."

"Woe to ye, pirate! I know ye now! Long John bespeaks Sam Bellamy."

"Long John! Long John!" cried Sam in relief. "Your master lies over the crest of the dune, the high dune by the sea. Wounded he lies in a hollowed-out cave. Go to him, brother! Go to him quickly, lest he die of his wound!"

"Whither away, pirate?"

"I make my way to the town."

" 'Tis a more westerly trail, pirate."

"Aye. Thankee, Long John."

The Indian disappeared in the night as swiftly as he had come.

2

Samantha's Ride

W HEN Long John found Caleb Snow, the wounded captain was so exhausted from loss of blood and exposure that as he made effort to tell the Indian about the wreck of the *Whidah,* the breath inside his breast failed him and he lapsed again into a faint. Long John lifted the Cape captain to his lean, strong-muscled back. With offsea winds to favor him, he made his way, bent nigh double, to the little house in the dunes. There Samantha undressed Caleb and put hot bricks at his feet and sides, but he lay groaning and out of his head in Jeremy's upstep bedroom. Once he roused briefly: "Jeremy?" he questioned. Samantha made no

180

answer. She raised his head with her hand behind it and put a warm posset to his lips.

For a while she and the Indian in silence sat beside the bed, and as the posset took its effect, warming, relaxing, soothing, Caleb fell into a sleep. Then Samantha gently unwound his head bandage and looked at the ugly wound.

" 'Tis too long exposed for me to stitch. You'd best go for the doctor, Long John. Though with all that has happened this terrible night, I doubt that he will come."

Long John nodded.

"Saddle the mare. If there's footway, ride her to the village. If the doctor's horse be too wearied to bear him, bid him ride back on the mare."

The rain had stopped, but the wind still blew. The door slammed shut behind Long John. Samantha returned to the bedside. Caleb, who suffered from a rising fever, began to mumble in his sleep, at first incoherently, then with short understandable phrases. From these Samantha drew forth the grave tidings that the *Abigail* was sunk, and that Caleb and the *Abigail's* crew had been made prisoner by pirates. Yet in some strange way he and Sam Bellamy seemed to have sailed a vessel, for he kept giving advice to Sam on the wayward course of the ship. Somewhat later, he relived in his mind the grim hour when the two captains climbed a cliff hand-over-hand, using spikes like the ones that led from Dune Valley down to

Jeremy's ledge. Gradually, as Samantha listened, she became aware that Caleb and Sam had separated somewhere on the dunes and that Sam Bellamy alone, unwounded, was wandering over the sands.

The Captain sank into deeper slumber. Samantha's thoughts turned to the Island, to Jeremy and Maria Hallett, imprisoned there by the storm. With a start of fear she recalled that Sam might never have heard of Caleb's house, built since he left the Dune Country. But he would of a surety have inquired of Maria, and learned that she lived on the Island. Undoubtedly he would head there.

Samantha leaned over the sleeping captain. She counted the even pace of his breath. She placed her hand on the throb of his pulse and nodded in satisfaction. Then with a quizzical glint in her eye she went to the cupboard in the pantry, fetched a bottle of Jamaica rum and placed it close to the bedside.

She took down from its peg by the chimney the Captain's loaded musket; then she paused to peer out of the window. Close-shuttered night encircled the house and the winds were loudly complaining. She lighted a staunch sea lantern, put on her go-to-meeting bonnet and her heavy wear-weather shawl.

Caleb was sunk in restoring sleep. He no longer put his hand to his head as if the pain of it roused him. Samantha touched his cheek with her hand, then went out of the door and down the path, with the lighted sea lantern in one hand, the heavy musket in the other. Outside the path by the posy fence stood the Indian pony, Seesaw.

"Well met, Seesaw," said Samantha Doane. "You can safely take me where I be going — though 'tis a curious thing," she mused, "what goes on in the wits of an Indian. Why should Long John leave his pony behind and ride the Captain's mare?"

Holding the lantern aloft in the wind, she inspected Seesaw more closely.

"Got a stone in your foot?" she inquired anxiously. For answer the pony turned his head and gazed at her with luminous eyes that shone in the lantern glow.

"Where's your saddle?" she demanded abruptly. "No bridle, neither, to guide ye. So Long John's been gambling his gear! 'Tis God's mystery how a praying Indian gets him a taste for dicing and rum along o' the Grace o' God.

"Bide where you be," she ordered the pony, and ran his broken halter rope into the iron ring of the hitching post.

She returned to the house and brought out of the door a sturdy ladderback chair. She unhitched Seesaw, tied the sea lantern to a lock of his mane, tucked her shawl ends into her belt and climbed up on the chair. Seesaw whinnied, pawed with his forehoof. "Set still," admonished Samantha. She lifted her skirts high in the air and flung a leg over his back.

With the musket balanced in front of her she gave a firm dig with her heels to the sleek sides of her mount. "Be off, Seesaw," said she.

Seesaw stood still. He turned his head till his eyes sought hers and Samantha's temper flared. "Quit turning your moon face round," said she. "Up anchor, Seesaw! Sail!"

She gave him a sharp rap on the flank with the butt of the heavy musket. Seesaw curvetted, arched his neck, but remained on the seashell path. Then, ten paces in front of him, knee-high from the ground a taper shone, a glimmering, wavering green light that seemed to beckon him on.

As if in answer to this strange summons, Seesaw started toward it. He followed it over the pine-tree hill and down to the edge of the swamp. There, the great storm had overturned trees, and hurled broken boughs into matted reeds. When Seesaw reached the edge of the marsh, he stopped and stiffened in protest.

"Git along, git along," Samantha urged, but the pony balked, and stamped his hoofs, and nearly slipped into a bogwallow. Then a small light glimmered over the shallows, over the flood of rippling tidewater that now concealed the bar.

Again the pony went forward, progressing steadily along a path submerged by the tidal flow. More than one light illumined the marshwater along this sunken bar.

"All manner of lanterns be out tonight," observed

Samantha soberly. "Trust ye to these, Seesaw? There
be evil here in the swamp."

She lifted her own sea lantern high. Around the
edges of its flickery light the darkness seemed impene-
trable, yet the pony, without guidance or rein, continued to splash ahead.

After Samantha had ridden thus for some half turn
of the hourglass, Seesaw came to a stop. Samantha
lifted the lantern again and peered through a gap in
the reeds. Bending over a deepwater pool, she perceived in the lantern shine an expanse where the water
glimmered softly, like a window lit from within. Below
on the sands a stalk-eyed lobster wove back and forth
in a curious dance like the mock of a minuet. In one
claw he clutched a pair of rusty lensless spectacles and
appeared to be staring at an open logbook which lay
on the sand beside him. He glanced up at Samantha
Doane, then backed away in a hurry. Up from the
deep came a resonant voice with a mournful note in
its tolling. "Spinster, *one!*" it boomed through the
night — "Spinster *riding on a Moon Pony!*"

"Giddap," said Samantha Doane severely with a
baleful glance at the lobster.

Again the low lights glimmered on the path and
Seesaw plodded on. The winds had died down to
occasional gusts and when Samantha reached the
Green Pool she surveyed its surface as best she could
with the lantern held over her head.

" 'Taint no pool, 'tis ocean," said she. "Lucky I be

I was trained in my youth to ford real rivers on a hoss."
She tugged briefly at the broken halter rope and Seesaw came to a standstill. "Bide a bit, Seesaw," said she.

She took off her bonnet, tore a string from it, put
the bonnet back on her head. She knotted the string
through the handle of the lantern and tied it to the
barrel of the gun. Then she took off her white necker-
chief and lifting up her numerous skirts she fastened
them round her middle. She adjusted herself to a good
knee grip and a well-balanced seat on the pony's bare-
back. Then with both hands holding the musket high,
she dug her heels into his flanks.

"Come along, Seesaw," she encouraged. "What I
have to say to your master, Long John, for gambling
your saddle and bridle away had best not be heard by
Parson Treat who sets sech store by Redmen."

Seesaw waded slowly into the wave-rocked, ice-cold
pool. There were no lights anywhere now in the marsh
save the lantern that swung precariously from the
barrel of the ancient gun. Soon the pony was swimming a sea current and Samantha, who like all Cape
women was well versed in the dangers and tricks of
fording a river on a horse, shifted her weight to windward or waveward when the gusts or the waves were
strong.

The pony swam on steadily till they reached the
center of the pool. Then he hesitated, began to plunge.

"Steady, Seesaw," said Samantha Doane, "there's a
blackhearted pirate gone before us, and none but a

boy and a girl to face him, not to mention a wappity dog."

Still Seesaw floundered.

"Ye're a peck o' nuisances!" Aunt Samantha lifted her voice and addressed loudly the shadows around the pool. "But from the Snow larder ye've filched fine vittles and ye've all of ye ridden our mare. 'Tis time ye gave aid to a friendly body. Light up them green-gold candles!"

As she spoke, a light shone far to the right. The pony swerved unexpectedly. Samantha's bonnet string broke and gave. The lantern fell away from the musket and sank in the Green Pool.

"Now ye've done it!" she scolded. "Ye rascally wet-foot tribe! Why couldn't ye give a hand with the lantern? Why couldn't ye light the path staunch and steady instead of behaving like a parcel o' fireflies scooting through a June night?"

Suddenly to her immense surprise the lantern reappeared on the surface of the Green Pool. It floated along, topside up, with its light undoused by the wetting. On the top of the lantern a figure was seated, its knees drawn up under its pointed chin, its dark eyes bright in the lantern shine, its feathered cap in its hand.

"Good eve to ye, Mistress Doane," it said in a clear, bell-like voice.

"So 'tis you, Ancient."

"Yea, Goodie."

"What have ye to say, Yorkshire bred as ye be, for this wayward offspring ye spawn?"

"Alas, Mistress Doane, they be not as we, the younger folk of our time."

"Fetch me my lantern back, Ancient. Ye were ever a thieving crew."

"I'll give it back to ye soon, Mistress, but now it must serve as the lead vessel for the fleet coming up with the guns." The Dobby grinned. He resettled his cap on the curls of his big-eared head.

"I've a mind to paddle ye here and now."

"But none to catch me, Goodie."

Drawing her brows down into a scowl Samantha fixed the Dobby with her piercing arrow-sharp gaze.

"Answer me forthright!" Her voice was stern. "Where is he who has brought us these sorrows? *Where is the Old Comer now?*"

"He lies on the sands of Nauset, Goodie, spewed forth by the knowful waters. He beats with his frail old hands on the earth that will not let him in."

"Ancient, is this man Lucifer's self?"

"Nay, mistress, but one of his ilk. Who gathers an host of rebel souls! Who would conquer Eden anew!"

As he spoke the first soft glow of the dawn enmisted the marsh and the island. The sea lantern grounded on a strip of shore and was promptly pulled upward, out of the tide, by three small dobbies who strained at the task like sailors heaving a dory.

"Ancient!" Samantha's voice caught in her throat, "how fares it now on the island?"

"Mistress, it fares but ill, I fear. There's not a sand-falling to lose. The dawn is coming, alack, alas, and we must leave ye, Goodie. Ride — ride — RIDE — " called the Dobby and his words sounded further and further away as the top of the sun shot over the rim of the white-capped thundering sea.

*   *   *

Those who have ridden on errands of war, to succor a life or to fly before fear, know how the eyes strain far ahead at the core of the road, at a twist or a turn, as if to devour its distance. Know how the forms of the night flash past in their sidewise, separate, passing worlds, sensed but uncomprehended.

So Samantha rode up the pine-tree path with the eyes of the Marsh Dwellers on her. The overhead boughs still cherished the night though the amber air was graying. Once a dark figure sprang swiftly aside and looked to be shaped like a man. Once the pony's hoofs flashed spark from stone. Once he stumbled and nearly pitched forward.

The lights of the greatroom shone through the trees, twin stars suffused with the morning. Samantha drove the pony straight toward the line of the lighted window. Then seizing his broken halter rope she reined him to a swerving halt. For a moment she peered through the salt-rimed bars, then lifted the ancient musket, thrust its muzzle between the bars and settled her hand to the trigger.

3

The Coming of the
Black Bellamy

WHEN Maria Hallett went out of the door into the
eye of the storm, Wu Wang the wolf rose from the
hearth, swayed to his feet, limped toward the door.
Jeremy drew it slowly open while his heart thumped in
his breast. As the halting, heavy gray body stumbled
across the doorstone, Jeremy hurled the door shut and
ran the bar through its hasp.

For a few moments he clung to the bar, his knees
giving way beneath him. Bimini came and nuzzled his
hand. Outside the hut the heavens were still, doubly
still, stiller than earth had ever seemed before.

190

Slowly Jeremy made his way across the greatroom to the hearth. The fire, shorn of its ember logs, lay scattered and needed rebuilding. He piled the hearth logs high. He filled with water a kettle that hung from the long hook on the crane. These two tasks every Cape boy was trained to do when danger threatened, in the days when a home was a place of strength that relied on its own resource.

Then Jeremy knelt before the hearth. He tried to pray, but words would not come, so he took Bimini close in his arms and boy and dog crouched together, staring into the flames.

They were startled by a clear, soft light as if many moons were shining, outside the tiny house. Lured by wonder, hesitant, fearful, the two made their way to the upstep bedroom where the light shone more brightly.

Outside, in the heart of a circular clearing, blue flames burned in the iron kettle into which Mistress Hallett, when she left the house, had placed the embers from the hearth. The Sea Witch knelt by the kettle. At first Jeremy thought that she knelt in prayer, then he perceived that her hands were not folded but held a small open book. In this she read by the light of the flames, and now and again she lifted her head as if to speak to the huddled clouds that fled through a crowded sky. The hood of the cloak fell back on her shoulders. Her long hair shone in the flickery light like a fountain of living gold. Jeremy thought how fair she was. A flash of pity, a stab of loyalty struck through his somber fear.

"She is passing fair," said he to his dog, "but not so lovely as my mother."

The dog quivered, pressed close to the boy.

The blue light slowly expanded till its searching fingers pierced through the aisles of the black-boled piny forest. There Jeremy saw the gleam of eyes, of at least a thousand watching eyes, large eyes, small eyes, slit eyes, yellow eyes, green eyes, small black beady eyes, staring, blinking, moving back and forth at the forest's shadowy rim.

Against the light from the cauldron, the body of Wu Wang the wolf was silhouetted sharply. Stretched on his haunches, his head held high, he had about him the heathenish look of the Sphinx in Egypt's desert.

Then Mistress Hallett flung into the cauldron the coin and the ring from her hand, and the two who watched at the window recoiled from a shock of light. A thundering force shot up in the air till it seemed to sever the sky. When again they dared to look through the bars, a thick, white, luminous cloud had mushroomed up into the heavens, where it lay like an old-time thick-petaled rose, set apart from the angry storm. And to it the trailing mists of the marsh clung like a drift of leafage.

Cloud and mist hung for a moment over the house in the forest. Then as if spurning the way of the winds, and the scudding stormheads above them, the cloud and the mist moved slowly seaward, over the tumbling ocean.

The blue light faded from the kettle. The eyes of the Marsh Dwellers vanished, and a sudden gust of wind-driven rain beat on the roof of the house. Jeremy heard Mistress Hallett's voice: "Let me in! Let me in, Jeremy!"

A hankering swept over him to leave the house door barred. Then he remembered how his own mother stood alone with Mistress Hallett when the goodwives stoned her away. He recalled how his father journeyed through winter winds and treacherous fog to fetch her needments and food. Quickly he unbarred the door.

Into the room the Sea Witch came, half fell, half stumbled. The wolf limped in after her and resumed his place by the fire. Slowly she made her way to the settle where she lay exhausted, her face so white, the shadows so dark beneath her eyes that Jeremy found that his heart was torn with a new pity and fear.

Maria saw the boy's concern. "Be not afeerd," she whispered, with a small encouraging smile. "I have done all that lies in my power to save your father's life."

Then she seemed to forget the child. She muttered to herself in soft, blurred tones. Jeremy could not catch all the words, but he heard her say, *"A ship for a ship! Old Comer, where is my soul?"*

Jeremy went to the cupboard. He brought forth

India tea. He put some into a kettle and steeped it well on the hearth. Carrying the tea-brew in his hand, he knelt beside the settle.

"Mistress Hallett," he said, "drink of this, a little. 'Tis what Aunt Samantha gives to us when we are ill at home."

Maria Hallett roused herself. She took the cup, sipped the hot strong tea. Color came creeping back to her cheeks. A soft light shone in her eyes. And Jeremy's heart went out to her, and all the sense of strangeness and fear vanished as thus he tended her.

"Mistress Hallett," he begged, "how shall we know whether my father lives or not? Can you not cast again a potion into the flames on the hearth?"

"Do not ask too much of me, boy," she said. "I have sold my heart's love for your father's life, lost power over the winds and tides, and over the small folk of the marsh who looked to me to guide them."

The storm increased in fierceness. Stones from the chimney thudded on the roof and rolled down its sloping pitch. The two by the fire sat in silence, the boy consumed by fear for his father, the woman drawn and exhausted yet as one who has supped from a cup of grace, and passed from the turbulence of youth to a time of more tranquil wisdom.

For a long time they sat together, humble and lonely and still, but each at deep peace with the other; and the boy's head fell against Maria's knee, and wearied by the long day and night, he closed his eyes in slumber.

Maria stroked his forehead. Now and again she bent to gaze at the small grave face whose dark-lashed eyes and pointed chin brought to her mind with such stabbing loss the long ago years with Abigail.

*   *   *

Suddenly the wolf raised his head. Bimini leaped to his feet and growled. A knock came at the door.

"Maria, Maria!" cried a man's voice.

Maria Hallett sprang to the door — swiftly she thrust back the bar. Into the room stumbled a tall, rain-drenched man. He was coatless, streaming with water. He put his arms up over his eyes as if the drip-torch blinded him.

"Maria," he whispered, and would have fallen, but Maria steadied him, and led him slowly to the settle beside the fire. There he sank down heavily, resting his head on his crossed arms that he laid on the end of the table.

For a few moments the room was still save for the heavy breathing of the man, the small movements of the anxious dog, the crackling sounds of the hearth fire.

"Sam," said Maria Hallett gently, "what fate has befallen the *Paradise Bird?* Where lies Captain Snow?"

"The *Whidah* is lost," Sam Bellamy said. "My men

lie dead on Eastham's shores or drift, flotsam in the tide!"

"And Caleb Snow?"

"He is safe, Maria. He lies on the Dune Before the Sea in a hollowed-out bed, to the leeward of the wind. Already Long John has gone to him. The Indian found me stumbling through the dunes and I sent him to succor his master."

The huge man lifted his head. He looked at the peaceful firelit room, at the quiet woman beside him.

"I have found ye," he whispered. The words sufficed till the sounds of the storm aroused them.

"I must go as I came! I must leave ye, Maria. Oh, how can I leave ye again?"

"I will hide you here on the island, Sam."

"The King's Men will follow my trail! I shall be hanged within flux of the sea — if I do not escape before Sun-coming!"

Maria seemed not to hear him. "I have clothes of my father's aloft, Sam. I will fetch them from the chest upladder."

"Hearken!" Sam's voice resumed courage and fire. "Before all else I would ye should know that I won for you the fairest treasure that ever was drawn from the sea. And the ship all seamen have longed to possess: the 'Paradise Bird,' the *Whidah!*"

"But the *Whidah* lies sunk on the bars, Sam."

"I have seven of her consort ships afloat; and must

make my way to the Province Lands, there to rejoin my fleet."

Maria gazed compassionately at the weary, bedraggled seaman. "Sam," she said, "it was ever thus. Either you alone must conquer the world, or forfeit it in death. I have no destiny save yours — nor have I any stomach, Sam, for the evil lot of the sea robbers."

As she spoke, the wolf raised his gaunt head and peered with blank eyes at the pirate. Sam Bellamy stared at the wolf.

"What manner of dog is this?" he demanded.

He sprang from his seat. The wolf rose.

"Be still, Wu Wang," said Maria Hallett, but the wolf uttered a low sharp growl. Slowly Sam Bellamy shifted his gaze from the blind wolf to the woman. A new note came in his voice.

"Maria, Maria, what do ye here? Here on this hidden island? Whence came this wolf? Whence the wild storm? Men say that you are a sea witch!"

Maria stood very still.

The man's voice rose, fear ridden, tense.

"Maria, is this tale true?"

"Aye, Sam," answered Maria Hallett. "I am the Sea Witch of Eastham. I sold my soul for the ship *Lilith*. I have bought it back with the *Whidah*."

"What talk is this?" Sam took a step backward. "Was it sorcery wrought from the Spell Books ye read, that drove the *Whidah* on the bars?"

"If that were true — "

"Then are ye damned! Doubly damned! In the eyes of the God in whose faith ye were raised! And untrue to the troth ye plighted!"

"Have you forgotten," said Maria drily, "who was in need of a ship?"

"Not at such price!"

"Have you forgotten who pledged to return to Eastham Parish to wed me with book and ring?"

"Have I not come — were it not for your sorcery — laden with treasure such as no man has seen since the sinking of the galleon?"

"Have you forgotten the souls of the sailors drowned in the cruel sea?"

"You shall pay for this with your life," said Sam. "No woman lives who abides on the land yet has power over ships at sea. Though I loved ye more than a king's ransom, if you have sunk the *Paradise Bird,* then for such sin you must die."

He sank down again on the settle and buried his head in his hands. Maria poured for him a cup of wine and placed it on the table but he only stared at it doubtfully and pushed it slowly aside.

Suddenly he raised his head. "Who is your lover now?" he cried. "Caleb! Aye, Caleb Snow! Him, like a fool, I pulled out of the ocean."

He laughed bitterly, briefly. "Think ye, Maria, I shall let Caleb, or Lucifer himself, possess you?"

She stood silent by the hearth. The pirate rose

from the settle. He took two unsteady steps toward her, and was brought up abruptly by a small whirlwind that pummeled him front and rear.

"Ods Bods!" said the huge captain, distracted into a quaint surprise, "what manner of thing is this?"

A sharp pain seared his leg as he stood surrounded by the raging fury of fighting boy and dog.

Sam seized the boy's wrists, flung him off his feet; then with the small arms pinioned firmly, looked into the boy's white face.

"Abigail!" he exclaimed astonished.

"Not Abigail," said Maria. "Abigail's son, Jeremy. Abigail died of a stoning."

Bimini still clung by his teeth to the pirate captain's leg.

"Call off your dog," said man to boy, but Jeremy clamped his own teeth together and spoke no word to Bimini.

"Jeremy," said Maria firmly, "have you not heard Sam tell us here that he saved your father's life? Pick up the dog in your arms, boy. Wait by the upstep bedroom. Let pass what must betwixt him and me. 'Tis not of your comprehending."

The Captain released the boy's arms. Jeremy stood, white and still, staring up at the drawn brows of the towering weary shipmaster.

"Have ye sunk my father's ship?" he asked.

"Aye," said the pirate, "she fought to the death."

"When I am grown," said Jeremy Snow, "I shall

seek you out and kill you. The *Abigail* was a fair ship.
Ye fought her with the guns uneven!"

Again Maria spoke to Jeremy. He lifted Bimini
from the floor and holding him tightly in the circle of
his arms, the boy sank down with his back to the wall.
Sam Bellamy rubbed his bleeding leg and returned
again to the settle. It seemed for a while as if the anger
and the fierceness had gone out of him.

"Drink your wine," said Maria quietly. "You have
need of strength and a warming. I will go aloft to my
father's sea chest and bring warm clothes and dry."

She climbed upladder to the loft. There Jeremy and
the Captain could hear her moving about. Sam slowly
drank the cup of wine and stared at the blazing fire.
With narrowed eyes, his gaze kept returning to the
eyes of the blind wolf. Now and again his glance rested
on the boy and dog by the door. After a while Maria
came downladder with an armful of heavy clothes, but
when she offered these to Sam, he murmured, "Lay
them by, for a time. A seaman is wont to be drenched
by the sea. He has no fear of a wetting."

Maria piled the clothes on a chair and turned to the
open larder. She was stopped by Sam Bellamy's voice.

"Maria!" he spoke in a tone of command. "Bring
the books from the jeweled chest."

She paused. "What would you with books, Sam?
You cannot read their tongue." She approached the
settle, gazed into Sam's eyes. "The books in the Spanish chest," said she, "must remain to the end of time.
They do not belong to me, Sam."

"Bring me the books," he persisted. "I will burn them, here, in the fire."

"They are not mine to give to ye, Sam. There remains no knowledge save these on earth of the spells which they record — knowledge that men have wrung with their lives from the moving forces of wind and tide, from the wheel-about stars, from the bowels of earth. These ye shall not destroy at your will to batten the fears of witchcraft."

Sam's voice was harsh with anger. "Give me the books of sorcery!"

Maria retreated slowly toward the door of the downstep bedroom beyond which, by the head of the bed, the jewels on the lid of the chest gleamed in the light of the fire.

"Think ye," said Sam, "that any man who has guided a ship on the oceans would let the traffic of the Seven Seas fall into the hands of a witch? Twice ye have tricked me. Twice betrayed me. I will destroy the sorcery!"

Maria Hallett reached her hand for the gun that had been her father's, that stood by the downstep door. Sam saw the move; he sprang toward her, and plunged his knife in her breast.

"Sam," she sighed, and fell forward. He caught her, held her close in his arms, then laid her down on the settle. For a few moments she seemed as in sleep, while man and boy, in moveless silence, grew equally breathless and still. Then she stirred, moaned, and over Sam's face crept the shipmaster look of courage. With steady hand and an even strength he drew the knife from the wound. A dark stain spread slowly over the bodice of her dress.

Jeremy's warning voice rang out: "The wolf, pirate! The wolf!" Sam turned. Wu Wang had gathered himself and crouched as if for a spring. Sam drove the knife deep in the wolf's shoulder and the gray beast sank down.

Stumbling, groping about with his hands, Sam made his way to the chest. He thrust back the lid, seized the ancient books, carried them across the greatroom and cast them into the fire.

Holding tightly to Bimini, Jeremy crept toward Maria's door and toward her father's gun. He was halted by the Captain's voice.

"Boy," said Sam, "leave the gun be. And tell the townsmen of Eastham Parish that the pirate, Samuel Bellamy, killed the Sea Witch of Eastham, that ships, whatever flag they fly, may sail true to the charted stars."

The books blazed in a sudden brightness. The fire leaped up on the hearth. The flames grew slowly transparent, and a drifting mist rose out of their depths and lay like delicate moonlight over Maria Hallett. For a moment Sam gazed down on her, then strode out into the night.

Jeremy's grip on his dog loosened. Bimini hurled himself against the door in an anguish of pursuit.

"No! No! Bimini!" cried Jeremy, and ran to fasten

the bar. Then he turned back where the Sea Witch lay, still and white on the settle. Seizing the shirt she had brought from the loft, he tried to staunch the flow of her blood. For a moment she opened her eyes and smiled.

"Mistress Hallett," said Jeremy, "shall I try to save some part of the books from the flame? Their magic words are vanishing fast but a few I might yet secure ye."

"'Tis of no matter," she whispered. "Their powers will come again — when man is more fitted to use them — when more fortunate stars convene."

A snarling sound brought Jeremy to his feet. The wolf, with the knife in his shoulder, crept toward the weaponless boy. A flash of white leaped through the air and clung to the wolf's neck. The gaunt head turned. Long yellow fangs tore at the dog's shoulder. Like a bundle of stained cloth Bimini was flung against the greatroom wall.

Then a terrible noise shook the little house like the thundering blast of a cannon. The wolf reared and fell by the hearth. A cloud of heavy acrid smoke sent Jeremy crouching by Maria.

Through the smoke a sharp voice spoke at the window: "Boy, unbar the door!"

*　　*　　*

Samantha Doane looked shrunken and old as she stood, silent, by the settle. She lifted Maria's hand in hers, then closed the hyacinth eyes.

Slowly she turned toward the boy. Jeremy knelt by the house wall, grief in his sagging shoulders. Now and again a tremor passed through him as he stared at the bleeding dog.

"Lift your dog slowly," said Samantha. "Lay him here on the table."

Tears rained down Jeremy's face. He lifted the limp body in his arms and placed it gently on the table. Samantha fetched water from the kettle. She tore off a strip of her petticoat, passed it swiftly through the steaming kettle water, wrung it endwise, staunched the bleeding. Then she tore a towel into long strips and with these bound the dog's shoulder.

"Now take your dog in your arms," said she. "'Tis the feel of his master a dog needs most."

As she spoke a quiver passed through the small body. Slowly Bimini lifted his head and licked Jeremy's chin.

*   *   *

When Long John and Caleb Snow reached the hut on the Island, Maria lay in the downstep bedroom. Candles burned at her head. She was dressed in her best, with her scarlet shawl folded neatly over her shoulders. The blue counterpane patterned with stars formed a coverlet over the bed. On a rug by the fire Jeremy slept, murmuring, stirring fitfully, his face still furrowed with a boy's first sorrow, his wounded dog in his arms. A shawl had been thrown over the body of the stiffening wolf.

"Samantha," said Caleb, "is the boy safe?"

"There he sleeps."

"What of Maria?"

"You had best look on her, Caleb. She has been stabbed to the death."

"By Sam, Samantha?"

"Aye, Caleb."

"Where is he now?"

"He has gone from here. The boy does not know where."

Caleb and Long John went with Samantha into the downstep bedroom. Maria's golden hair was braided as Samantha had been wont to braid it many long years ago. One braid hung down by the bedside and almost reached to the floor. Another braid shone golden on the coverlet of stars.

"She was the fairest woman," said Caleb, "in the Colony of the Americas. 'Tis an ill destiny, this."

"Her mind was too quick," said Samantha Doane. "It tripped folk up. She read too much — it addled her wits with folly! But I'd rather be loved by Maria Hallett than sit to the right of the Lord."

Long John drew from his deerskin coat a knife with the curious symbol of a bird carved into its handle. He lifted the knife to his forehead, then with the point of it drew a circle lightly on Maria's brow.

"Nay, Long John," admonished the Captain, "leave be revenge — 'tis not our province. Sam Bellamy was neither as wicked a man as men hereafter shall say of him — nor as brave — nor as foolish."

The three returned to the greatroom. There Captain Snow took note of the rug humped up beside the hearth. "What lies here, Samantha?" he asked as he drew the rug to one side.

"'Tis her wolf. I shot him through the window. He went wild at Maria's death, Caleb. He meant to kill the boy."

"Ye shot him?" Captain Snow was puzzled. "With what gun, Samantha?"

"With your musket, Caleb."

The Cape captain faced her. "Samantha, how did you find your way through the marsh in the midst of the storm? How did you swim through the Green Pool? 'Tis nigh an ocean yet!"

His eyes sharpened; his voice rose in pitch: "*How did you swim through the Green Pool with your bodice dry, and your petticoats dry, and the powder dry in the gun?*"

"I had me a mount," said Samantha Doane, as she slanted her gaze toward the floor. "Long John rode the mare to the town, Caleb, but he left Seesaw by the gate. 'Twas the pony brought me safely through the storm. *I rode him through the Green Pool!*"

The lids of Long John's eyes drooped. He spoke in a low tone. "Seesaw maddened," said the Indian. "Seesaw died on the Great Beach on the night of the full moon."

Epilogue
on
the Dunes

Epilogue on the Dunes

THERE ARE many tales in Eastham about Maria Hallett. There are tales of the Black Bellamy. Toward the end he returned, men say, to Higgins Tavern and died there, down in the Apple Tree Hollow.

Jeremy Snow became a great captain and lived in Hallett House. Bimini lies buried on the Dune Before the Sea.

And if of a night when the fogs roll in you walk along the Great Beach, you may hear the pounding of tiny hooves. Then step aside from the frothy edge of the ocean. Make way for something pixie, goblin, boggart, something mischievous and moon-touched galloping through the night. Perhaps if you are quick of eye, you will catch a glimpse of a silver mane blown back like shredded fog. Behind it, look sharp for the rider, for keen little eyes, huge flapping ears and a feather in a red cap!

But do not search for the Secret Island that once rose, like the dark center of a golden flower, in the midst of a shimmering marsh. In a great sea storm the island sank and the rising waters covered it, and now no one will ever know whether or not the Marsh Dwellers there spoke the speech of man.

Now, as then, the mutinous winds rise from the timeless sea. And man reweaves his curious spells: potions that alter the aspects of life; flames that mirror the shining wakes of moving vessels at sea. By alchemies secret and potent, he severs lodestone and star. But this knowledge that comes with the turn of the wheel man has rewon to his sorrow. Ill fit for the use thereof, he moves in a mooncast again.